"What is it, Lori?
Why are you afraid?"

Rick frowned at her, as if puzzled at her fear. "Surely you're not afraid of this?"

His face swooped down toward hers. His lips pressed against hers. For a moment Lori was still, not knowing what to do. Then incredibly something seemed to burst open inside her, the way the petals of a flower burst out of their sepals when at last they feel the warmth of the sun. Her lips trembled and parted at the soft seductive touch of his, and she swayed against him, her eyes closing.

Rick made an exclamation against her mouth, and his arms went around her, crushing her slender body against the rocklike hardness of his own. Keeping hold of her, he stepped sideways, and they both sank onto the bed, until they were lying across it....

Books by Flora Kidd

Harlequin Presents

Harlequin Romances

These books may be available at your local bookseller.

For a free catalog listing all titles currently available,
send your name and address to:

Harlequin Reader Service
2504 West Southern Avenue, Tempe, AZ 85282
Canadian address: Stratford, Ontario N5A 6W2

FLORA KIDD

tropical tempest

Harlequin Books

TORONTO • NEW YORK • LONDON
AMSTERDAM • PARIS • SYDNEY • HAMBURG
STOCKHOLM • ATHENS • TOKYO • MILAN

Harlequin Presents first edition November 1983
ISBN 0-373-10643-2

Original hardcover edition published in 1983
by Mills & Boon Limited

CHAPTER ONE

THE weather was warm and sunny. Little puffs of white cloud rolled lazily across the bright blue sky. Yellow light glittered on hard-baked tarmac and on the outspread wings of big jet-planes and tiny island-hoppers. Inside the small departure lounge in the airport terminal building on the Caribbean island of Sint Maarten the air was hot and humid. Sweat was beginning to shine on the faces of some of the many travellers who were crammed into the room waiting to go aboard the various planes.

Over the intercom system a voice made an announcement several times, presumably in more than one language. As far as Lori Stevens was concerned the announcer could have been speaking double Dutch, because she couldn't hear or understand one word. There was too much noise coming from the engines of the planes outside and too many people were talking or shouting inside. Noise and confusion seemed to be the order of the day.

Lori glanced at her watch. Nine-twenty. In ten minutes' time the plane for the island of Dorada was scheduled to take off, and the announcement could have been about that. She looked around anxiously, searching for someone who looked official that she could ask. There seemed to be no one except the tall black woman wearing the uniform of an air stewardess who had just come in from outside and was shouting that the flight for Miami and New York was ready for boarding. She had hardly finished speaking when most of the people who were crammed into the waiting room and who were, apparently, American holidaymakers, surged towards the doorway.

Another muffled unintelligible announcement came over the intercom. Really worried now in case she was going to miss the plane for Dorada, Lori looked around again at the few people who were seated near to her.

Directly opposite to her was a young couple. They were holding hands and looking into each other's eyes, oblivious to everyone else, so obviously lovers or honeymooners that Lori let her glance slide past them rapidly. A year ago she could have been sitting in an airport like this with Mark. A year ago today she and Mark might have been waiting for a plane to take them to an island where they had chosen to spend the rest of their honeymoon. Only Mark had been killed the day after their wedding day. . . .

Dragging her thoughts back from the disastrous path along which they were heading, she looked at the black man sitting next to the young couple. His hands were folded placidly across his stomach and his eyes were closed. Not much help forthcoming from him. Her glance drifted on to the man who sat next to him whom she had noticed before and who now seemed to be drawing something on a pad of paper which rested against one bent up knee.

As she stared at him, hesitating to speak to him

because, to her way of thinking, he looked rather disreputable with his longish brown, blond-streaked hair and faded blue denim shirt and jeans, his eyelids flicked up and he looked right at her with wide-set greenish-grey eyes; eyes the colour of the sea on a wild and windy day.

'Now why the hell did you have to move?' he said rather sharply.

'Me?' exclaimed Lori, sitting up straight and giving him a disdainful glance. 'Are you talking to me?'

'Who else?' he retorted. 'Now don't look at me, look at the doorway, the way you were before.'

'Why?' she demanded. 'Why should I look at the doorway?'

'Can't you see?' he replied impatiently, lifting the pad of paper from his knee and shaking it at her. 'I'm trying to sketch you. Another few minutes and I'd have finished—but you had to move. Now look back at the door.'

'But you have no right to sketch me,' Lori protested. 'I don't want to be sketched by you.' As she had guessed just from looking at his square suntanned face and husky physique, he was the sort of man she detested—rude, over-bearing and careless of other people's opinions.

'Too late. You have been sketched by me. Except for your chin and shoulders.' He grinned suddenly, long well-shaped lips curving back over straight white teeth, cool sea-green eyes glinting with amusement. 'You would like to have a chin, wouldn't you? Now look towards the door, please. Just for a few minutes.'

She could have stood up and walked away, but

the room was so small and crowded it would be difficult to escape from him. She gave him a slow assessing glance. The cool greenish eyes returned her gaze mockingly.

'I'll do what you ask only if you'll tell me if the flight to Dorada has been announced yet. I couldn't understand what the announcer was saying just now, and I don't want to miss the flight,' she said.

'No one ever can understand what she says,' he remarked dryly. 'So you're going to Dorada? Travelling alone?' he queried.

'Yes.' She spoke shortly, determined to keep him at a distance.

'On holiday?'

'No. I ... I'm going to work there.'

'Really?' His eyebrows went up in surprise. 'Where? I'd no idea that there were any jobs available on the island for non-natives.'

'It's a private arrangement. I'm going to work for Mrs Bernice Alden for six months,' Lori replied as stiffly as she could, wishing she hadn't got into conversation with him. 'About the flight to Dorada,' she reminded him.

'It hasn't been announced yet,' he replied.

'But it's scheduled to leave in exactly two minutes, at nine-thirty!' Lori exclaimed, looking at her watch.

'Scheduled is right,' he drawled. 'But that doesn't mean it will take off on time. Don't worry about it. You're in the Caribbean now, where no one ever hurries. You'll catch the plane to Dorada. I'm going there too, so when I leave you'll know it's time to board the plane, but I expect Chuck Williams, the second pilot, will come to tell us when to go aboard. Now will you look towards the door, please?'

'Oh, all right,' she muttered rather ungraciously, and turned her head so that she could look at the door. A sudden thought occurred to her and she turned her head quickly to look at him again. Immediately he roared at her,

'Look towards the door, dammit!'

'But how do I know you're right about the flight to Dorada?' she complained.

'You just have to trust me,' he retorted, glaring at her.

With a toss of her head she looked back at the door, feeling blood rush into her cheeks as she realised that the young couple and the thin black man who had seemed to be asleep were all looking at her and were laughing.

'He's right about the flight to Dorada, ma'am.' The black man came over to stand before her. 'The plane has to wait until all the bigger planes have taken off. But don't worry, all of us sitting over here are going to Dorada. You just come along with us when we go out.'

'Thank you,' she said, holding herself straight and still and never looking away from the doorway. She didn't want to be roared at by the brute in blue denim again.

'You're welcome, ma'am. And don't you mind about Rick drawing your picture. He's always drawing someone and something. He's even made sketches of me serving in the bar at a hotel near Denny's Beach where I work. He's a great artist and. . . .'

'You talk too much, Sylvester,' said the man in blue denim abrasively. 'And you're blocking my view. Get out of the way.'

'Okay, I'm moving, I'm moving,' replied Sylvester, returning to his seat. 'But just you make a good drawing of the lady. She sure is pretty!'

Embarrassed by the black man's outright compliment, Lori continued to stare at the doorway through which bright sunlight slanted, wondering why the man called Rick had decided to sketch her, of all the people in the waiting room. It wasn't as if her looks were uncommon. There was nothing striking about her profile. Her only claim to beauty was her hair, which was long and thick, with a slight wave in it, a rich dark brown in colour, glinting with golden lights in the sunshine.

More people came into the lounge. Another air stewardess appeared in the doorway and announced that she had come for passengers flying to Antigua and Barbados. People surged towards the door and out. A few minutes later a man in a blue uniform entered and said in a soft lilting island voice that the plane for Dorada was ready for boarding.

Lori turned her head slowly and cautiously to glance at the man in blue denim. He looked up, nodded at her and sitting up began to stuff his sketching pad into a canvas shoulder bag. Lori collected her bag and her raincoat and followed the young couple to the doorway. After looking at her boarding pass the man in the uniform directed her towards the small silver plane which stood on the runway about a hundred yards away and to which the young couple were already walking. Lori stepped out into the bright hot sunshine, hastily pushing her sunglasses on.

The plane was the smallest she had ever flown on and had sixteen single seats arranged on either side of a central aisle. Her seat was the front one on the right and she could see into the cockpit where the pilot was sitting leaning his arms on the instrument panel in front of him and staring out at the runway. When everyone was settled in their seats, the second pilot, who acted as steward as well and had directed them all to board the plane, gave them instructions as to what they should do in case of an emergency, wished them all a good flight and went to take his seat in the cockpit, closing the door after him.

Lori looked over her shoulder back at the other passengers. The young couple sat immediately behind her and were holding hands across the aisle. Behind the young man sat Sylvester and he was talking to another black man who sat in the seat across the aisle from him. Two more people sat behind them and the man called Rick who had sketched her was in the last seat on the left.

The plane took off and climbed slowly but steadily into the air, flying out across the harbour of Phillipsburg towards the sea. Leaning back in her seat, Lori looked out of the window beside her and watched the play of sunlight and shadow on the deep blue, almost purple water below, feeling excitement pulse through her because she was on the last stage of the journey which had brought her all the way from the port city on the east coast of Canada where she had been born and had lived all of her twenty-three years until yesterday.

From snow, ice and fog, from the dreary grey streets of the city, from the desolate snow-covered countryside around it, she had been wafted south to warmth and sunshine, to palm trees and yellow sands. And now, instead of sitting at her desk in the History Department of the old museum building in her home town where she had worked as a secretary-typist for the past year, she was sitting on this little plane, swooping over the tropical sea, flitting through sunlit gauzy clouds, glimpsing exotic mountain-ous islands, dark blue shapes seeming to float in the sun-shimmered distance.

It was incredible, like a dream come true. And yet she had hesitated to come, had been afraid to leave the protective shell she had built around herself ever since Mark had been killed. She had almost turned down Bernice Alden's invitation to come out to Dorada and work for her for six months.

If it hadn't been for Kathy Nolan, her close friend with whom she had shared a small apartment on the west side of the city, she wouldn't be here now. It was Kathy who had urged her to come.

'Who is this Bernice Alden? Where did you meet her?' Kathy had asked after Lori had told her about Bernice's offer of a job one evening as they had been eating their evening meal in the living room of their apartment.

'She's a historian. She was born here and

educated here and for a while she was a professor of history at the university, but some years ago she married Harvey Alden, after his first wife died. You must have heard of him,' Lori had replied.

'Who hasn't around here?' Kathy had agreed. 'The local millionaire who started a small lumber business and ended up practically owning the province. But he retired years ago and his sons direct the Alden company now. Didn't he go to live on an island somewhere in the Caribbean?'

'That's right. It's called Dorada, and Bernice went to live there with him.'

'How old is she?' the lively, inquisitive Kathy had asked next.

'Oh, about sixty, I would think.'

'Mmm. She was quite a bit younger than him, then. He must have been over eighty when he died. Why do you think she married him? Was it for his money, do you suppose?'

'I don't know,' Lori had replied. 'And I don't really care. She's a lovely person, and for the past few months while she's been visiting her step-children here in the city she's been studying every day in the museum, looking up the records of the trade that went on between the Canadian Maritime Provinces and the Caribbean islands during the nineteenth century. You see, she's writing a history of Dorada and the other sugar islands. I've been helping her to search for the information she needs and we've become quite friendly.'

'And now she wants you to go to Dorada with her and help her write the book,' Kathy had contributed, nodding her curly head. 'You're going to go, of course,' she had added. 'You must! It's a chance of a lifetime and will be good for you, much better than staying here moping about and feeling sorry for yourself.'

'I don't mope and I'm not sorry for myself,' Lori had protested, cut to the quick by her friend's honest remarks.

'Well, you have to admit you haven't been the life and soul of any party since Mark was killed,' Kathy had retorted. 'You haven't gone anywhere, met anyone new or joined in any sort of group activity. . . .'

'Because I haven't wanted to,' Lori had interrupted angrily.

'Anyone would think you're the only woman who has ever lost her husband soon after she married him, the way you've behaved,' Kathy had continued. 'Well, I've news for you. You're not the first nor the last to be cheated by death. Accidents often happen to newlyweds. I heard only the other day about a bridegroom who collapsed and died after his wedding, and. . . .'

'I don't want to hear. I don't want to hear!' Lori had cried out. 'I know I'm not the only woman it's ever happened to, but knowing that hasn't made it any easier for me to adjust. I loved Mark. . . .'

'Did you? Are you sure?' Kathy had jeered. 'Are you sure it wasn't just infatuation for a father figure, the older successful man who could provide you with everything you'd always longed for?'

'How can you say such horrible things!' Lori

had almost shouted, more roused than she had been for a long time. 'We were in love and we had everything planned for our life together. It was going to be perfect. That was why it was such a shock when he went out that morning, from the hotel where we'd stayed the night . . . and he . . . he . . . didn't come back.'

'That's it. That's what was wrong. It was going to be too perfect,' Kathy had retorted, not seeming in the least upset by Lori's distress.

'What do you mean?' Lori had demanded, stiffening up.

'It was too much like the story of Cinderella, with you as Cinders, the poor little orphan girl rescued from poverty and the tedium of a nine-to-five job by the handsome Prince Charming who also happened to be your boss. Oh, it was all so neat and tidy . . . and dull, so dull. Nothing romantic about it at all.'

'I thought there was,' Lori had replied stubbornly. 'And I like things to be neat and tidy. So did Mark.' She had stared at Kathy. 'You never liked him,' she accused.

'Because I thought he didn't care about you, really care about you as a person, I mean. He cared only about himself, and he saw how you could contribute even further to his creature comforts by keeping his house, cooking his meals, entertaining his business associates.' Kathy had given Lori a pitying glance. 'You know why Prince Charming chose Cinderella rather than her stepsisters, don't you? He could see she was much better at keeping house than they were.'

'That isn't why Mark married me,' said Lori,

still stubbornly defensive of her marriage. 'And I
... I still can't believe he ... he's dead. That's
why I don't go out anywhere to meet anyone else.
I'm always hoping he'll come back, that the
doorbell will ring and he'll be standing there
when I open the door.'

'Morbid, that's what you are,' Kathy had said,
shuddering a little. 'And you know where you're
headed if you go on thinking like that? You're
heading for a nervous breakdown.'

She had left her seat suddenly and had rushed
round the small table to fling herself on her knees
beside Lori and to put her arms about her.

'Oh, Lori, I don't want to quarrel with you,'
she had whispered, 'but I've wanted to say all
this for some time. You're letting your regrets for
what might have been destroy you. You've let
this mourning for Mark go on too long. Have you
looked at yourself lately? Have you seen how thin
you are, how drawn your face is? You're not the
girl Mark Stevens knew and married. He
wouldn't know you now even if he did come
back. Can't you see what you've been doing this
past year? You've given up living just because he
was knocked down and killed by a car as he
crossed a street. You've let him come between
you and life. For God's sake don't let him come
between you and this job Bernice Alden has
offered you. Don't let him kill you!'

'I ... I ... know you mean well,' Lori had
admitted. 'But I'm not sure ... if I can do what
Mrs Alden wants. I mean, I'm only a typist and
secretary. I know nothing about history, even
though I work in the History Department.'

'Let her be the judge of whether you can help her or not,' Kathy had advised. 'She must know what you're capable of or she wouldn't have offered the job to you. You've got to take it, Lori. You've got to go, and maybe you'll have a torrid affair in the tropics with some suntanned playboy who'll teach you to have fun and live it up for a while so that you'll get Mark out of your system for ever.'

'Me? Have an affair with a playboy?' Lori had said, laughing a little, glad that the conversation had become less serious. 'Oh, no, that sort of thing isn't for me.'

'How do you know it isn't?' Kathy had argued. 'Have you ever tried having an affair?'

'You know I haven't,' Lori had retorted. 'I'm not like you.' She knew that Kathy had had an affair. 'Mark was the only man I've . . . I've ever known physically,' she had admitted in a whisper. One night she had spent with him, their wedding night, and it hadn't been the most successful of matings. It hadn't been what she had hoped for or imagined. There had been nothing ecstatic or fulfilling about it, but she would never have admitted that, not even to Kathy.

'He's the only one you've known, and the only one you're likely to have known if you go on the way you are, shutting yourself up in this apartment, cutting yourself off from people and life,' Kathy had said scathingly. 'Oh, Lori, for your own sake take this job Bernice Alden has offered to you. When do you have to tell her?'

'Tomorrow. She leaves for Dorada the day after. If I agree to go she'll make arrangements for me to fly to Dorada as soon as I can be released from my job at the Museum. But the job won't be for long and I'll have to come back here to look for another job six months from now.'

'So what? If you go it will be a marvellous experience. And what have you got to lose by going? Nothing, only your job at that fusty, dusty old museum.'

Kathy had gone out that evening and there had been no more discussion between them, but the argument between them had roused Lori so much that she hadn't been able to stop thinking about herself and how she had seemed to her friend ever since Mark's death. In the mirror in the small bedroom she had studied her appearance and had seen how pale she had become, how droopy and wistful-looking. Sorry for herself. It was that accusation of Kathy's which had hurt most. Orphaned at an early age, brought up first in an orphanage and then by loving but strict foster-parents until she had been old enough to go to work, she had never felt sorry for herself but had always prided herself on her positive outlook on life.

Yet secretly she had dreamed of romance, of one day finding an ideal man to love with whom she could spend the rest of her life. She had believed Mark to have been that ideal, so that when death had snatched him from her she had been devastated as all her dreams for their future together had been shattered and she had sunk into despondency.

She had been surprised at herself; surprised she had let it happen, and all that night she had thought about what Kathy had said to her, eventually coming to the conclusion that her friend had been right. She had been letting her regrets for what might have been come between her and life. It was time she pushed Mark and the future they had planned together out of her mind. It was time she struck out on her own, left the city where she had always lived, the people she had always known, and went adventuring.

The next day she had given notice to her boss at the Museum and had told Bernice Alden she would go to Dorada and work for her. Bernice had been delighted, and the arrangements had been made for Lori to join her on Dorada at the beginning of March. And so here she was on the second day of March, close to her destination.

Lori glanced out of the window again, and was startled. Very close to her destination—too close. The tree-covered slopes of a mountain were sliding past the window, so near that it seemed that if she had been able to open the window she could have reached out and touched the leaves of the trees. Gasping, she looked down and saw wicked-looking jagged rocks jutting up through trailing streamers of white cloud. Where was the plane going? She looked round wildly to see if anyone else was disturbed by the closeness of the plane to the mountain. Only the young couple behind her seemed worried. Holding hands still, they were also gasping and staring out of the window. The rest of the passengers were relaxed in their seats, not even bothering to look out.

Suddenly the sound of the plane's engine changed and the plane banked in a steep curve

away from the mountain. Beneath her Lori saw
some land, bright green against the blue water, a
narrow peninsula pushing out into the sea and
crossed by a runway. Then the plane seemed to
be falling straight down towards the sea. She
closed her eyes and held her breath, hearing the
young woman behind her shriek. After a while
there was a jolt. She opened her eyes. The plane
was on the runway and was taxiing towards the
red-roofed shack which was the terminal building.

Last off the plane, Lori followed the other
passengers towards the building. The air was
warm. Palm trees swayed in the steady trade
wind and the sunshine was hot on the back of her
head and her neck. By the time she reached the
building her pantyhose were sticking to her legs,
her feet felt too big for her shoes and she was
wishing she could take off the jacket of her suit.

Inside the building she waited behind the
young couple to show her passport to a
uniformed immigration officer who stood at a
counter under a sign which said all visitors to the
island should go that way. The other people off
the plane, who were presumably all residents on
the island, had walked right through into the
lounge area and were picking up their luggage
which had been brought from the plane.

After she had had her passport checked Lori
went over to the luggage, picked up her two cases
and carried them to the Customs officer who was
waiting near the exit. In a few minutes she was
stepping through a doorway and was out in the
sunshine again.

'Taxi, ma'am?' Several voices chorused at her and she found she was surrounded by several brown-skinned men, all dressed in brightly coloured shirts and pants and all of them grinning hopefully at her.

'No, thank you. I think someone has come to meet me,' she said, remembering Bernice Alden's instructions about what she should do when she arrived at Dorada airport.

'All right, ma'am.' They all took the news cheerfully and scattered, going back to their cabs which were parked in a line a few yards away.

Lori put her cases down and took off her suit jacket. She looked about her and caught sight of a tall wide-shouldered figure in blue denim. The man called Rick was standing beside a small white jeep-like vehicle. Standing close to him was a tall blonde woman who was dressed in a length of brilliantly printed cotton which was wound round her slender body like a sarong, leaving her golden-skinned shoulders bare. The woman was smiling up at the man in blue denim and one of her hands was playing intimately with the opening of his shirt where it was unbuttoned.

Slowly the man in blue denim turned his head and looked at Lori. Raising a hand, he pointed at her. The blonde woman looked at Lori, stared for a few seconds through the big sunglasses she was wearing, then turning to the man said something and laughed. Lori had the most uncomfortable feeling the woman was laughing at her, and she turned away to look in another direction, searching for Bernice Alden's tall distinguished figure and curly white hair.

A few seconds later an attractively husky female voice drawled beside her,

'Excuse me. I believe you're Lori Stevens.'

Lori turned. The blonde woman was there, sunglasses hanging from one hand, and was looking down at her with hard glass-blue eyes.

'Yes, I am,' she replied.

'I'm Tracy Alden. Bernice asked me to come and meet you and to drive you to Tamarind—she isn't feeling too well today. Is this all your luggage?'

'Yes.'

'No, don't carry it. I'm sure Rick will do that for you,' said Tracy Alden, turning to look in the direction of the white jeep. But it wasn't there, nor was the man called Rick. 'Damn!' muttered Tracy, her teeth snapping together viciously. 'He's gone!' She turned back to Lori, her rather full lips pouting sulkily. 'He's our nearest neighbour at Tamarind. You may have heard of him. He's Patrick Greville, the sculptor. He's just come back from New York where he's been giving a seminar on sculpture with some other well-known artists. He's really moving up in the world of art and will be famous one day for his ability to portray human emotions in stone.'

'No, I haven't heard of him,' replied Lori. 'I don't know anything about American artists,' she added, picking up her cases. Tracy didn't seem at all disposed to carry one of them.

'Rick isn't an American,' replied Tracy. 'He's a citizen of Dorada now. God knows where he's from originally. The car is over here.' She strolled gracefully across the sun-baked tarmac and Lori followed her, lugging her suitcases, feeling the sweat running down her body inside her clothing.

The car was big and elegant, blue in colour. Lori put her cases in the boot and then they both slid into the front seats. The road from the airport zigzagged in a series of hairpin bends up the side of the mountain Lori had seen from the plane and then divided into two.

'I'm going to take you round the windward side of the island, the side that faces the Atlantic,' Tracy announced, taking the left fork. 'It's the least inhabited side, but it's the quickest way to Tamarind.'

Downhill the road dipped between unkempt sugar-cane fields and through a small village of wooden shacks where small brown and cream goats nibbled at the wayside grass and the scarlet flowers of poinciana trees and the purple blossom of bougainvillaea added exotic touches of colour to gardens bursting with coconut and banana palms.

On the outskirts of the village they met children in uniform, returning home from school, Tracy informed Lori, after being in class since early morning. The girls wore grey skirts, white blouses and long white socks and the boys were all in grey shorts, white shirts and long white socks. Some of them, mischief lighting up their shiny brown faces with wide white grins and glinting eyes, stood right in the path of the car until it was almost up to them before jumping out of the way; playing 'chicken', a game they played with anyone they suspected of being a visitor to the island, Tracy said.

Away from the village the road swept close to the shore beside a long beach of pale yellow sand against which long rollers of white surf crashed. Beyond the surf the ocean stretched, brilliantly blue, tossed by the steady trade wind into white-capped waves, perpetually moving.

'This is Denny's Beach,' said Tracy. 'There's a hotel here where all sorts of strange people stay. I think some of them are hiding from the law in their own countries.' Her laugh was a low gurgle. 'My stuffy father-in-law calls it a den of vice and a sink of iniquity. Personally I've had more fun there than I've ever had in *his* house!'

A building loomed up on the left. It was built right on the beach. Painted blue with white shutters at its windows, it was shaded by palms and casuarinas.

'There was a man on the plane who said he worked in the bar at that hotel,' said Lori.

'That would be Sylvester,' replied Tracy, nodding. 'I noticed he came out of the terminal building with Rick.' She glanced sideways at the hotel as they passed it. 'I expect that's where Rick is now,' she added sulkily. 'He would rather hobnob with people like Sylvester and have a drink in the bar there than come to Tamarind with us for a drink in civilised surroundings. I guess Bernice has told you all about Tamarind.'

'No, not really.'

'It's beautiful. The sugar planter who built it in the eighteenth century was one of the wise ones and built his home above the sandfly level, on the side of the mountain where the breezes blow away the mosquitoes. And Harvey Alden, my husband's grandfather, must have spent a fortune turning it into the ideal holiday hideaway, putting in a modern kitchen, adding an outdoor swimming pool, re-surfacing the old tennis courts.' Tracy glanced at Lori curiously. 'You're from the same city where Harvey Alden was born, aren't you?'

'Yes, I am. I've lived there all my life until now.'

'I lived there last year,' said Tracy with a little shudder. 'With my husband Ken Alden. We have a house on the river. It's supposed to be beyond the fog. Ugh, I hated it! I was so bored and lonely I began to misbehave myself.' Her mouth widened into a mocking grin. 'Then Clarke, Ken's father, laid down the law, said he wasn't going to let me drag the name of Alden in the mud, and he sent Ken and me down here. To become reconciled, he said.' Tracy gave a little trill of laughter. 'Last month Ken had to go back home to work and make more money, of course. Clarke cracked the whip and back Ken went to do his duty. I decided to stay here—much more fun.' She glanced sideways again at Lori. 'Have I shocked you?' she taunted. 'Are you a stiff-necked East Coast puritan like the Aldens?'

Lori didn't answer. She was too interested in looking at a building which had appeared on the right side of the road. Made of stone, darkened by the growth of moss, it had been ravaged by time. It was without a roof and the glass had gone from the windows. Weeds and bushes grew over the flight of steps going up to the gaping hole which had once been the front door. Goats grazed what had been an elegant lawn. Behind the ruin, higher up on the slope of the mountainside, towered a circular building, its restored walls built of glowing pinkish gold stone.

'What was that place?' Lori asked, looking back over her shoulder in an attempt to get another glimpse of the ruined house.

'Part of the old Greville plantation. Rick lives there, in the sugar mill, the tower you can see behind the house,' replied Tracy, slowing the car down to take a bend in the road which began to climb up away from the coast.

'What happened to the house? Why is it in ruins?' asked Lori.

'The story goes that the Greville who first owned the plantation built that house for his daughter on the occasion of her marriage to his best friend. But she never lived in it.'

'Why not?'

'From all accounts the marriage was one of those arranged affairs, and the man whom she really loved and who loved her became furiously jealous and challenged the bridegroom to a duel on the wedding day. Both men were fatally hurt in the duel and died. The girl threw herself out of the upper window of the house and died too when she heard that she'd lost both husband and lover. The house was locked, sealed and abandoned, and no one has ever lived there from that day until Rick turned up nearly eight years ago and moved into the sugar mill.' Tracy laughed again mockingly. 'She must have been crazy! I can't believe any woman in her right mind would behave like that today just because two men had gotten themselves killed, can you?'

'Yes, I can. I can imagine it very easily,' whispered Lori. 'But what about the original Greville house? Is that in ruins too?'

'No. The original Greville house is Tamarind,' replied Tracy. 'And we're almost there.'

The car turned off the main road on to a smoothly surfaced narrow road which led straight to two big stone gateposts. The gate was open and Tracy drove in, circled round a flowerbed and stopped the car in the shade of trees. As she had said, the house was beautiful, built of blocks of pinkish brown stone. Its plain sash windows were edged by black and white shutters and under a spiderweb fanlight the panelled black door had a brass knob and knocker.

'I'll get one of the servants to take your luggage in,' said Tracy, stepping out of the car. 'We'll go round to the back of the house. I expect Bernice is sitting on the terrace.'

Leaving her jacket and raincoat in the car, Lori followed the striding Tracy up some shallow steps and along a stone pathway past some long windows overlooking a garden bursting with exotic-looking flowering shrubs and around another corner, up some more steps on to a wide stone terrace with a roof that was supported by stone pillars around which leafy vines twined. At a small table Bernice Alden was sitting, her left leg propped up on another chair, and she was reading.

'Here she is, your Girl Friday, Granny Bernice,' Tracy sang out.

'How nice to see you, Lori!' smiled Bernice, putting down the sheaf of papers she had been reading. 'Forgive me if I don't get up, I have a very sore leg to-day, a touch of thrombosis. Do come and sit down. I expect you're hot and are longing for a cold drink.' She picked up a small brass handbell which was on the table and rang it sharply three times. Lori sat down on a chair, wishing she could take off all her clothes. Never had she felt so uncomfortably hot.

'Don't order any lunch for me, Granny Bernice,' said Tracy. 'I'm going out again right now. See you!'

'Where? Where are you going?' demanded Bernice, calling after Tracy, who was striding away.

'To Denny's Hotel,' the blonde woman called back. 'I've got a date to meet someone there.'

'Who? Tracy, come back at once!' demanded Bernice rather breathlessly. 'How many times must I ask you not to go to that place?'

'You can stop asking, Granny, because I'm not going to stop going,' retorted Tracy, and jumping down the steps she disappeared round the side of the house.

Bernice sighed and leaned back in her chair, her lined face wearing an anxious expression, her lips twitching, her eyelids flickering. She looked at Lori and shook her head.

'I don't know what to do,' she complained. 'Tracy is my stepson's wife. They've been married for only eighteen months and already their marriage is on the rocks. And it's Tracy's fault. They came here for a holiday in January and now she won't leave. And she will associate with the most impossible people. She's formed a sort of attachment for the disreputable artist who lives on the other part of the estate. Poses for him in the nude, I shouldn't wonder.' Bernice sighed heavily again. 'I wish she'd go away, back to Ken or even back to her own family. She's driving me to distraction! I can't concentrate on my work.'

'I'm sorry,' mumbled Lori, who didn't really know what to say. Already the strange beauty of her new surroundings was having an effect on her. The scents of many flowers wafted on the refreshing breeze and many birds were singing in the garden or swooping about the terrace. It was quiet, peaceful, relaxing. She could have sat there all day doing nothing quite easily, and she didn't want to know about such a disruptive person as Tracy Alden seemed to be. 'This is a lovely place,' she said.

'You're right, it is,' said Bernice, the frown fading from her face. 'And I shouldn't bother you with my troubles so soon after your arrival. Ah, here's Johnson.' A thin black youth, wearing a bright blue shirt and white pants, appeared. He walked gracefully towards them, swinging a tray in one hand. 'Now what would you like to drink, Lori?' asked Bernice. 'Some fruit punch made with coconut juice? I can assure you it's a very refreshing drink the way that Johnson makes it.'

'It sounds good,' replied Lori.

'Bring two of your punches, Johnson,' Bernice asked the boy pleasantly. 'What has Lily made for lunch to-day?'

'Seafood salad, wholewheat rolls and strawberry cheesecake,' replied Johnson, twirling his tray skilfully into the air and catching it behind his back before sauntering away, wiggling in time to some tune which must have been going through his mind.

'You'll find the food excellent,' said Bernice. 'Almost everything is home-made and much of the fruit and vegetables are grown in the garden here.' She smiled at Lori, her hazel eyes twinkling. 'I'm really very glad you're here, you know. I think we're going to get on well with the history. You're just the sort of person I need to help me—quiet and calm, unflappable.'

'Thank you,' replied Lori sincerely. 'And I'm very glad to be here.'

CHAPTER TWO

LORI removed the sheet of paper on which she had been typing, together with the carbon paper and yellow copy paper, from the typewriter. Sitting back in her chair at the desk in the pleasant book-lined room which Bernice Alden had made into a study, she read through what she had typed, checked it for mistakes. That morning, about ten days after she had arrived in Dorada, she had begun to type the opening chapter of Bernice's history of Dorada and the other sugar islands, and she felt as if she was doing something of importance at last.

When she had finished reading the page she laid it carefully on top of the pile of pages she had already typed that morning, placed the copy on top of the pile of copies and put the carbon paper away in a drawer in the desk. It was noon, time for her to stop work for the next few hours while the sun was at its highest and the temperature at its hottest. Later in the afternoon, when it became cooler, she would start typing again and would work probably until seven o'clock, when dusk would fall quite suddenly and dramatically and the sky would become dark purple pricked with bright stars.

The study was on the cool northern side of the old stone house and from the window in front of her desk she had a view of the remains of the

31

original Greville sugar mill. Built of the same pinkish-brown stone as the house, it was round, like an inverted cone which had had the top cut off. Its roof had gone and its arched doorway no longer had a door. Glowing in the sunlight, surrounded by tropical plants and trees, it was a memorial to when Tamarind had been a successful sugar plantation.

'At one time huge sails of canvas fixed to wooden vanes were attached to the wooden upper part of the tower,' Bernice had told her when she had asked the historian how the mill had worked. 'On the other side from the sails there was a long wooden pole reaching to the ground. A mule was hitched to the pole or boom, as it was called, and as the mule walked round the tower the wooden part rotated so that the wind vanes and sails faced the wind.'

'But what were the sails for?' Lori had asked.

'To provide power using the wind. As the sails spun the wooden vanes activated gears or wheels inside the mill which turned iron rollers that had been brought from England by ship. The sugar cane was crushed by the rollers until the juice ran out of it into troughs which led to a shed where there were large kettles heated by burning *bagasse*, the remains of the crushed sugar stalks.'

'Why was the juice heated?'

'To thicken it, and then it was ladled into slatted wooden trays to cool. The molasses dripped away through the slats, leaving *muscovado*, raw sugar crystals which were dark like molasses and tasted the same.'

'Like the brown sugar we sometimes use

now?' Lori had asked.

'Something like it, yes. Once every estate made sugar in the same way and kept itself and its workers supplied with sugar as well as exporting it to other countries. But now we buy it in paper bags at the grocery stores like everyone else,' Bernice had sighed for times past. 'And the mills are idle and falling into ruins and the people who once owned the plantations have all gone away.'

'What happened to the Grevilles who used to own Tamarind?' Lori had enquired.

'They all went back to England, but they kept this house as a holiday residence, a place to spend the winter in. Then the family became impoverished and the house was closed up. Just before the last world war the estate was divided into two and this part with the house was sold to an American who wanted a house on a Caribbean island. He carried out many of the renovations, restoring the stone walls, the windows and the roof. When he died it was put up for sale again and Harvey bought it.' Bernice's eyes had grown dreamy and rather sad. 'Harvey loved it, spent hours planning the garden and lived here for the last fifteen years of his life.'

'And the other part of the estate?' Lori had prompted. 'Was it sold too?'

'No. It seemed no one wanted the ruins of a haunted house,' Bernice had replied dryly. 'Not even the Greville who inherited. He didn't even come to see it. No one came near it until that artist fellow arrived and moved into the sugar mill and put a roof on it. He claims to be a Greville and a direct descendant of Robert Greville who built this house, but I don't believe him.'

'Oh. Why not?'

'I've traced the Greville family right back to their roots in England. Robert Greville was an aristocrat, the second son of an earl, who was sent out here by his father to make his fortune. There's nothing aristocratic about the man who lives in the other sugar mill. From all accounts he's an adventurer, who has seen a piece of property no one else seems to want and has taken it over. Everything about him is suspicious, especially his arrival in Dorada.'

'How did he arrive?' asked Lori.

'He came in a sailing boat, with a friend, from Mexico. It was stormy at the time and the boat was wrecked on a reef off the coast. The two of them waded ashore at dead of night. The man who calls himself Greville had nothing with him except the clothes he was wearing and a waterproof bag in which he carried some artist's materials, paint-brushes and tubes of paint,' said Bernice caustically. 'The next thing we knew he was living in the sugar mill behind the ruins and turning out paintings of local scenes and local characters and selling them to tourists in the market place in Williamstown.' Bernice had almost snorted with disgust, and Lori had been forced to hide her secret admiration of Rick Greville's will to survive in a hostile environment.

'He refused to move when he was asked by my husband,' Bernice went on. 'And he's been a thorn in our side ever since. We have nothing to do with him if we can help it. I hope you won't either, Lori, while you're here. He isn't at all respectable.'

Lori hadn't seen Rick Greville since she had arrived on the island, but she had seen some of his paintings on sale in the small capital of Dorada which was also the chief port, and she had admired his skill in capturing the beauty of local scenes in both watercolours and oils. But his best paintings, to her mind, were of people; of a group of native women selling their garden produce in the old broken-down market building; of an old man selling ice to visiting yachtsmen at the harbour; of Sylvester leaning on the bar in Denny's Hotel.

'Lori.' Bernice spoke behind her, bringing her back to the study, and she swung round on her typist's chair to face the older woman, who had just come into the room. Wearing a blue linen suit, a shady white hat and white gloves, Bernice was obviously going out. 'How did it go this morning?' she asked, coming over to the desk.

'I've typed ten pages. I don't think I've made any mistakes,' Lori replied. 'Perhaps you'd like to look them over.'

'Later. Maybe this evening,' said Bernice. 'I'm going to lunch with Admiral Bisset and his wife. He's a most interesting and informative old man. He commanded a warship in the Royal Navy at one time and he's quite an authority on the naval warfare in the Caribbean during the eighteenth century and has actually written a book about the time when Nelson was at English Harbour in Antigua. I don't expect to be back until about five, so why don't you take the rest of the day off? I'm sure you deserve a rest. You've worked so hard since you came. I'm really very pleased with what you've done.'

'Thank you,' said Lori. 'Enjoy your lunch.'

When Bernice had gone Lori put the cover on her typewriter and left the study. She went up to her bedroom, a pleasant room which faced east and had a view of the land sloping down to the distant glinting ocean.

For a while she stood at the window looking out. Ever since she had arrived in Dorada the weather had been good, especially up here on the mountainside at Tamarind where the trade wind blew incessantly, acting as a natural air-conditioner, keeping the temperature comfortable even on the hottest of days. But to-day there was a difference. The air was very humid and big clouds were piling up over the ocean and rolling steadily towards the island.

She had all afternoon free. She could do anything she liked—not that there was much to do at Tamarind apart from swimming, walking or just loafing about and reading. Well, she would go swimming first, before lunch. Turning away from the window, she stripped off her clothes, glad to peel them from her perspiring skin. Taking her one-piece black swimsuit from a drawer, she pulled it on. From the clothes closet she took out a white terry-towelling beach robe and a pair of rubber flip-flops. She stepped into the flip-flops, draped the robe over one arm, then left the room and went downstairs, going out of the house by the side door which opened directly into the garden.

The stone-flagged pathway twisted between

luxuriantly growing flowering shrubs and trees; spiky-leaved oleanders decorated with clusters of rose-coloured fluted blossoms; flame-coloured hibiscus flowers; reddish-purple velvety tails of the chenille plant hanging from heart-shaped leaves, and everywhere the thick swordlike mottled leaves of sanseviera.

She had learned the names of many of the plants from Lesley Carter, the amiable native Doradian employed by the Aldens to look after the big garden. He was the husband of the equally amiable Lily Carter who presided over the kitchen and produced delicious meals regularly with apparently little effort. With the help of their son Johnson and their married daughter Maureen, who came from the village of Coconut Point where she lived, to clean the house every day, Lesley and Lily kept Tamarind and its grounds in perfect condition both inside and outside.

Reaching the pool, Lori tossed her wrap over the back of a chair beside one of the round wrought iron tables, kicked off her flip-flops and walked to the edge of the concrete apron. As usual at that time of the day she had the place to herself. All traces of the barbecue dinner party which had taken place beside the pool the previous evening had been removed and no one would suspect that about forty people had been there, talking and laughing, eating and drinking, swimming and dancing and generally fooling around.

Lori looked down at her wavering image in the dimpling sun-flecked water. Then she glanced down at her bare arms. She had acquired an even golden tan during the hours she had spent every day at the pool. At last she was looking less like something which had lived under a stone, not so skinny and white, she thought with a little grin of self-mockery, and lifting her arms before she dived swiftly and cleanly into the water, rising to the surface in the middle of the pool.

The water was soft and tepid, refreshing on her hot skin. She swam two lengths, then turned on to her back to float, her eyes closed against the glare of the sun, kicking her legs occasionally so that she wouldn't sink.

It was the height of luxury for her to be able to walk out of the house where she was working and living and to dive into this pool. But then all Tamarind was luxurious to someone like herself who had never lived in such a beautiful house and had never stayed on a tropical island, and she would never cease to thank her lucky stars ... as well as Bernice Alden, of course ... for having been given the opportunity to come and stay on Dorada.

Even the presence of the restless and abrasive Tracy Alden hadn't irked her so far. In fact she found the blonde woman, so different in every way from herself, rather fascinating, and she was always wondering what Tracy would do next to annoy the staid and elderly Bernice.

Last evening's dinner party had been Tracy's latest piece of defiance. Without consulting Bernice she had invited her friends and acquaintances to dinner. They had all been extremely happy and noisy and had stayed until the early hours of the morning. There had been some local musicians present, two guitarists and a drummer and everyone had danced to the rhythmical Caribbean beat. Offended by the behaviour of some of the guests, Bernice had retired to her suite of rooms, but, persuaded by Tracy, Lori had stayed and had danced, and had to admit she had enjoyed herself.

Enjoyment, having fun, living it up, seemed to be Tracy's aim in life. She seemed to be driven by a demon to extravagant and reckless behaviour. She didn't behave like a married woman at all, or at least not as Lori imagined a married woman should behave. She behaved as if she weren't married—as if she had never vowed to cherish and love Ken Alden at all.

'He's so boring. All the Aldens are,' Tracy had confided one evening to Lori when she had returned from the hotel at Denny's Beach, slightly the worse for drink. 'All they think about is making money. Old Harvey Alden was a strict taskmaster and a great believer in the work ethic, and he brought his two sons up to be the same. And they in turn have brought up *their* sons the same. They like their women to be submissive, to stay in the background and keep house and produce children, more Aldens to carry on the dynasty. And I'm not like that.'

'Then why did you marry Ken?' Lori had asked.

'God knows,' Tracy had groaned. 'Because he's rich, I suppose, and I'm used to having money. But I didn't realise he would be so mean . . . or so under the influence of his father, Clarke Alden. I wish I could find some reason to divorce Ken so that he would have to pay me a huge amount in alimony. But he never puts a foot wrong—never. None of them ever do. I think they have ice in their veins instead of blood!'

Lori rolled over on to her stomach and swam to the end of the pool. Turning swiftly as if she were participating in a race and using the fast crawl which had once won her a trophy for free-style swimming when she had been a teenager, she swam the full length of the pool again.

As she pulled herself up out of the pool she was surprised to hear the sound of slow hand-clapping. Standing up, she shook her wet hair back behind her shoulders and looked round. Tracy was sitting by one of the tables. Dressed in tennis white, her long bare golden-skinned legs stretched before her, her blonde hair glowing like a halo around her head, she was sipping one of Johnson's strong rum punches through a straw. On the other side of the table, under the shade of the striped umbrella, also drinking a planter's punch, sat Rick Greville, seeming bigger than ever in casual white T-shirt and faded cut-off jean shorts.

'I'd never have guessed that you'd be such a fantastic swimmer, Girl Friday,' said Tracy, mockery rippling through her husky voice. 'She's so quiet and well behaved,' she added, turning to Rick. 'Never speaks unless she's spoken to. Quite repressed and inhibited!'

As luck would have it, Lori had left her beach robe draped over one of the chairs at the table, between Tracy and Rick, and her flip-flops were now under the table, otherwise she might have ignored Tracy's provocative remarks and gone on her way to the house. Slowly she approached the table, aware that every movement she made was being watched by Rick Greville.

'Where did you learn to swim like that?' Tracy asked.

'At home, in the pool at the Y.W.C.A.,' Lori replied shortly, picking up her wrap and slipping it on.

'Lori comes from the same part of the world as Ken, actually from the same city,' Tracy explained to Rick. 'Oh, I forgot, you two haven't been introduced, have you, even though you met at Sint Maarten airport. Rick, meet Lori Stevens. *Mrs* Lori Stevens. She's helping Granny Bernice write her history of Dorada. Lori, meet Rick Greville, artist, sculptor, and God alone knows what else.'

Lori glanced shyly at Rick and nodded at him. He nodded back, his sea-green eyes narrowing slightly as their glance drifted over her slowly. In order to avoid that cool appraisal she bent quickly to retrieve her flip-flops from under the table.

'That reminds me,' Tracy went on. She didn't like silence and could never wait for anyone else to speak, had to fill any void in the conversation with her own deliberately provocative chatter. 'I've been meaning to ask you, Lori, about Mr Stevens, your husband. What have you done with him? Have you dumped him? Are you separated from him? Or is he one of those rare liberated men who allows his wife to do her own thing where and when she likes?'

'Mark died a year ago,' said Lori quietly, sliding her feet into her flip-flops.

'Too bad,' murmured Rick, and she flicked another glance at him. She hadn't expected any sympathy from him, even as casually expressed as he had expressed it. He was still staring at her, but there was warmth in his eyes now. He was seeing her as a person now, not just a series of shapes, circles, triangles, ellipses, whatever it was artists saw that other people didn't see.

'I wish Ken would die,' Tracy said suddenly and harshly. 'I wish he'd die and leave me his money.' She picked up her glass and drank what was left of the rum punch.

'Now, Tracy, watch it,' drawled Rick. 'You're letting your claws show. That isn't the sort of thing a wife should say about her husband, and I'm sure you've shocked Lori.'

'Oh, she's easily shocked,' retorted Tracy, her words slurring together slightly. She had been quite tight at the end of the party the previous evening and didn't seem to have recovered. 'She's like the Aldens. She has a lump of stone instead of a heart, and ice in her veins. They've all got ice in their veins instead of blood. It comes of growing up in a place that's frozen for nearly four months of the year, I shouldn't wonder. They don't know how to live, how to love. They're not like us, Rick darling.' She stretched a hand across the table to cover one of his which was resting on top of the table.

'Missus Tracy.' Johnson had appeared on silent feet. He had been running and was slightly out of breath. 'Missus Tracy, come quick to the house! There's a phone call for you, long-distance.'

'Damn,' said Tracy. 'I expect it's my mother calling from Tampa. She's on holiday there.' She rose to her feet. 'Now don't go away, Rick. It's taken me a long time to entice you to Tamarind, and now that you're here I want you to see what you were done out of when this half of the Greville estate was sold.'

She went off with long easy hip-swaying strides. Lori took a few tentative steps away from the table as if to follow her.

'How did he die?' Rick spoke abruptly, startling her, and she swung round to face him. Leaning forward, one hand around the tall glass in front of him, he was staring at her again. 'Your husband, I mean,' he added.

'He was knocked down by a car when he was crossing a street,' she replied woodenly.

'How long had you been married?'

'Not quite twenty-four hours.'

'Good God!' he exclaimed. 'That's hardly any time at all. When did it happen?'

'A year ago. Excuse me.' She began to move away again.

'Don't go yet,' he ordered. 'I came here this morning to see you.'

'Me? Why?' She turned to face him again. Much to her annoyance she felt her cheeks grow warm and her heart skip a beat, rather foolishly, she thought, but it was a long time since a man had told her he wanted to see her again.

'I've been thinking about you a lot since I first

saw you in Sint Maarten,' he went on matter-of-factly.

'You ... you have?' Lori could hardly believe her ears. Was it possible he was making a pass at her? Slowly she sank down on to the chair Tracy had vacated and stared at him, her dark brown eyes wide. The sea-green eyes returned her gaze. They were cool again, surveying her objectively, sizing her up.

'And I've decided that you're exactly right for something I've had in mind for some time. But I had to see you again to make sure,' he continued. 'I'd like to do some more sketches of you, not just head and shoulders but all of you, in different positions.'

'Oh?' She was aware of a strange sense of disappointment because his interest in her was after all purely professional. 'Here? Now?' she queried.

'No. In my studio. It's in the sugar mill on the other half of the Greville estate.' His glance swept over her again. 'I'd need to see all of you,' he added pointedly.

'You mean I'd have to pose in the nude?' she gasped. 'Then the answer is no,' she added coolly, and stood up. 'I couldn't do anything like that. I'm sorry, but I can't do what you ask.'

'What do you mean, you can't do it?' he demanded, frowning at her. 'Of course you can. You're the most natural model I've seen for years. Your figure ... what I've seen of it ... is perfectly proportioned and you're able to sit still without moving for more than ten minutes. That's why I was able to sketch you at the Sint Maarten airport.'

'You had no right to sketch me,' she retorted. 'You never asked my permission. And I haven't seen your sketch. It could be terrible for all I know, a mess.'

He gave her a scathing underbrowed glance.

'I don't make "terrible" sketches,' he replied coldly. 'And it isn't a mess. But if you want to see it why don't you come over to my studio? Any time. This afternoon if you like, and I'll sketch you some more. A few hours of your time are all I ask, and I'd pay you the going rate for models in American dollars.'

'No.' Lori backed away. 'I don't have the time. I can't do it. Why don't you ask Tracy to pose for you?'

'Because she can't sit still for two minutes together,' he said dryly. 'And her figure isn't suitable. She's too flat-chested and her legs are too long, I'd never ask her to pose for me. She'd want to take advantage of the situation. And here she comes.' He gave Lori another sharp glance. 'I'll pay you double the going rate if you'll do as I ask.'

'No, no—I can't.' Lori shook her head.

'Wouldn't you know it was Ken calling, checking up on me!' exclaimed Tracy, flinging herself down on a chair again and reaching for the packet of cigarettes she had left on the table. 'He's on his way here,' she said, pouting. 'He'll be here this time tomorrow.' She clutched her bright head between her hands. 'Oh God, what am I going to do, Rick? He's threatening me with a divorce. Someone has been telling tales about me to him. He says he's got grounds.'

Seeing a chance to escape, Lori walked quietly away towards the house, guessing that Tracy wouldn't notice her leaving and that Rick would make no attempt to detain her while Tracy was there. The cool shadowy walls of the house closed about her, a haven from the oppressive heat outside. The weather was deteriorating, threatening a storm, and she felt uneasy for the first time since she had come to Dorada, disturbed by the hint of violence in the air and more than disturbed by Rick Greville's demand that she should pose in the nude for him.

In her bedroom she stripped off her swimsuit. From the mirrors in the room, the triple one on the dressing table and the long one on the door of the clothes closet, the reflection of her naked body seemed to mock her. Going over to the longer mirror, she studied herself, her glance lingering on her full tiptilted breasts, her narrow waist, her outcurving hips sloping down to her strong muscular swimmer's thighs. Perfectly proportioned, Rick Greville had said.

Colour flamed in her cheeks as she realised how closely he had been observing her, and she stared again at her reflection trying to see what he had seen or rather what he would have seen if she had agreed to pose for him in the nude. Her face grew even redder and with an exclamation of irritation she opened the closet door, swinging it wide so that she could no longer see herself. Reaching into the closet, she took out a plain wraparound cotton skirt and a white short-sleeved blouse and began to dress.

She lunched by herself in the small dining

room near the kitchen, then returned to her room, intending to read and rest as she usually did in the hottest part of the day. But after a while, realising she wasn't concentrating on her book, that her thoughts kept wandering to Tracy and then to Rick, she put the book aside and picking up the white cotton sunhat she wandered out of the house, thinking a walk would help her to sort out her thoughts.

Idly she strolled in the direction of the pool. The table where Tracy and Rick had been sitting was deserted. Staring at the empty glasses, the cigarette butts in the ashtray, the abandoned half-empty packet of cigarettes, Lori realised with a little shock of surprise that she had gone that way hoping Rick would still be there. She had been hoping to see him again.

Why? To tell him she would pose for him after all? Oh no, surely not. Then why? She wandered on past the pool along a path which led through the kitchen garden and up the hillside at the back of the house where sugar-cane grew wild, not really looking where she was going as she tried to analyse her own behaviour.

Why did she hope to see Rick again? He wasn't the sort of man who usually attracted her. For one thing, he was an artist, and she had always considered artists to be unreliable, unconventional persons, selfish, putting their art first always, and so far Rick had fitted in with her rather prejudiced view. And it was prejudice, she admitted ruefully, because she had never known any artists and she didn't know much about him. She only knew what Tracy and Bernice had told her about him.

Finding herself suddenly very hot and short of breath, she stopped walking and looked about her. She had climbed quite a long way and had an excellent view of the tawny green land sloping down in front of her to the edge of the sea. To her right the roof of Tamarind twinkled in the hazy sunlight through the foliage of its clustering trees and to the left, lower down the hillside, the stone walls of another sugar mill glowed softly. Unlike the mill behind Tamarind it wasn't in ruins. A cone-shaped roof of red tiles covered it and there was a window set at the back of it, high up, as if a room had been made in the upper part of the building. Below it, closer to the road, gaunt and dark, the ruins of its chimneys jutting up, was the house which had been built for the Greville daughter.

The path seemed to lead straight across a disused canefield past the mill and down to the road, and although the clouds which hovered over the crater of Dorado's volcano, Mount Brimstone, were threatening rain, Lori decided to go as far as the ruined house, satisfy her curiosity about it and then walk back to Tamarind along the road.

It took longer than she had expected to reach the sugar mill even though the going was downhill, and she paused to rest for a moment against the trunk of a coconut palm. A wide pathway led up to the steps of the mill and the battered-looking white jeep-like vehicle was parked on it. White paint trimmed the window which had been let into the thick wall above the arched entrance and the front door had been painted green. Spears of chaconia or wild poinsettia, scarlet and green, swayed in the wind against the stone walls and purple bougainvillaea twined up the railings on one side of the steps. On the grass on either side of the path two goats grazed.

A sudden gust of wind tugged at Lori's hair and twitched at her skirt, reminding her not to linger, and turning away, she began to hurry down the narrow gravel road towards the ruined house. By the time she reached the broken walls rain was falling heavily, sweeping in a grey curtain across the land.

The house itself provided no shelter, being only a shell without a roof with weeds and bushes growing where there had once been floors. But next to it there was a small square building; an outhouse in good condition with a corrugated iron roof. Its one window had been boarded up, but its door hung open, swinging creakily on its hinges. Lori dashed up the flight of stone steps to the doorway and stepped inside.

The room was dim, the only light coming through the open door, but she could see it was used as a storage place for gardening tools. There were also some boards of masonite resting against one of the walls. A strange swishing sound drew her attention back to the door. A wild gust of wind was sweeping through the trees. Suddenly the door swung and slammed shut. Trapped in darkness, Lori inched her way forward, her hands outstretched before her. Her fingers scrabbled against rough wood, searching for a knob or a latch, but there was none. She pushed hard against the door, hoping it might open. It didn't budge. Stepping back, she flung all her weight against it. Still it didn't open.

Feeling sweat prick her skin, she strained to see the door in the darkness, hearing thunder crashing overhead. Again she went forward and felt all over the door. There seemed to be no way of opening it from the inside. Swinging a leg back, she kicked the door as hard as she could. Nothing happened, so she flung herself against it again. It didn't even rattle.

Breathing hard from her exertions, she pushed her hair back from her damp brow, wishing the room was not quite so dark. Tentatively she moved about, her arms outstretched. Perhaps if she could find a suitable gardening tool she would be able to attack either the door or the boards at the window aperture. There must be an axe amongst the clutter of tools she had seen. There had to be an axe.

Ten minutes or so later, after walking into and knocking down the gardening tools and searching through them with her hands, she had come to the conclusion that there was no axe. Cautiously she felt the edge of a Dutch hoe she had found. Perhaps if she could slip it between two of the boards which covered the window opening she might be able to force them apart. The chances of success were not great, but it was all she could think of doing.

Some time later, it seemed like an hour, drenched in sweat and gasping for breath in the warm airless room, Lori flung the hoe from her and sank down on the floor. She had tried to pry the window boards apart and had failed. Rain was still rattling on the iron roof and thunder was still rumbling, but the worst of the swift tropical storm seemed to be over.

How long she sat on the floor, trying to summon the strength to make another attack on the door, she had no way of knowing, because she wasn't wearing her watch, and even if she had had it on her wrist she wouldn't have been able see it because the figures on the dial were not luminous. Slowly she got to her feet and after making sure she knew where the door was she began to attack it, using the handle of a garden spade as a sort of battering ram.

After a while, when she had succeeded only in exhausting herself, she dropped the spade to the floor and sat down again. She was so tired, as well as being thirsty, so short of air that she was beginning to feel lightheaded.

How often did Rick Greville come this way? Did he use the shed? Somebody did, and whoever it was had been already today and had inadvertently left the door open or hadn't closed it properly.

Lori groaned and wiped the sweat from her face with a corner of her wraparound skirt. She could be here until tomorrow, until whoever used the shed for storage came for something. She could be there longer than that. She could be there for days in the hot darkness, slowly becoming dehydrated as sweat poured out of her, slowly losing weight, slowly smothering through lack of fresh air, slowly dying. . . .

Panic streaked through her, giving her new

strength, and bounding to her feet she hurled herself at the door again, pounding on it with her fists and shouting at the top of her voice.

'Help, help me! Oh, please open the door and let me out! Please, please! Help, help!'

She shouted and beat on the door for as long as she had breath and then collapsed, coughing and choking, sliding down the door to lie in a heap on the floor without moving for a long time, vaguely aware that she must conserve what little energy she had left.

Time passed as she floated in and out of consciousness, sometimes acutely aware of where she was, sometimes sunk in a sort of stupor, hazily indifferent to the darkness, the heat and the smell of goat. Later, much later, she was roused by the sound of thumping on the door. A voice shouted,

'Anyone in there?'

Groggily she sat up and tried to shout back, but her throat was so dry her voice came out merely as a croaking whisper.

'Okay.' The voice was recognisable now as Rick Greville's, and Lori made a supreme effort to drag herself up by the jamb of the doorway until she was standing or rather swaying on her feet. 'Now, I'm going to show you fellows once and for all there's no ghost in here and there never has been.'

The door didn't open immediately. He had to tug at it, but at last it swung back and Lori was almost blinded by the bright beam of a flash light that lit up her pale face. At once two voices let out howls of terror and Rick exclaimed, 'What the hell are you doing in there?'

'I ... I ... I....' Lori croaked, and moved forward. Her knees gave way beneath her and her head reeled, but before she fell he caught her in his arms and held her closely.

'How long have you been in there?' he demanded, but she was incapable of speaking and could only move her head negatively against his shoulder. Vaguely she heard other voices, boys' voices speaking with the island lilt, asking questions. Rick's reply was crisp yet mocking.

'So I was wrong and you were right. There was someone in here. But she'd no ghost. I can tell you that. And she's much heavier than I ever imagined she would be. Now you two, go back home and tell your father what we found.' Lori felt his fingers grope under her chin, lifting it so he could see her face. 'Listen, Lori, can you hear me?' he asked softly, and his warm breath feathered her cheek. Again she couldn't speak, but she managed to nod. 'I'm going to take you to my studio. Can you walk?'

With his arm about her waist supporting her she managed to walk down the steps, but when they reached the ground everything seemed to whirl around her again and she clung to him, feeling she might faint.

'No, you can't walk,' Rick said dryly. 'So it looks like I'll have to carry you. Now this won't be very comfortable, Lori, but it's the best I can do.'

He lifted her and threw her across one shoulder in a fireman's lift and began to walk. Her head wagged from side to side and she lost consciousness. She came round as he was opening another door and knew when he had laid her down on something springy yet soft in a brightly lit room. Thankful that she was no longer in the dark lying on a hard floor, she tried to sit up and failed. Her head felt as if it were stuffed with cotton wool and she had a raging thirst.

'Water,' she croaked. 'Please.'

'Right here,' said a voice, and she looked up to see Rick standing beside her, a glass of water in one hand. He knelt down close to her, and pushing his other hand under her neck raised her head, then held the glass to her lips. 'Easy does it,' he warned. 'A sip at a time.'

Never had water tasted so good to Lori, and slowly, her intake controlled by Rick, she drank every drop in the glass. When she had finished he removed his arm from behind her head and let her lie back against the cushions.

'How do you feel now?' he asked.

'A little better, thank you.' Her voice was still weak, but at least it could be heard. 'What time is it?'

'Twelve-thirty . . . midnight,' he replied.

'Oh, no!' she exclaimed, struggling into a sitting position. 'It can't be that late!'

'But it is,' he drawled, lifting up from his knees and sitting on the edge of the couch close to her. 'What were you doing in that shed, and how did you get in there?'

She told him, and when she had finished her explanation added in a whisper,

'I must have been in there for more than nine hours. Oh, it was awful! I thought no one would ever come. I thought I was going to die!' She broke down, reliving the horror of those sweat-drenched, thirst-racked hours, and buried her face in her hands. 'I was terrified,' she sobbed. 'Nothing like that has ever happened to me before. I . . . I . . . thought I would die in there!'

Rick put his arms around her and drew her against him, to comfort her.

'Did you shout for help?' he asked.

'Yes,' she sniffed into his shoulder. Under her cheek the cotton of his shirt was smooth. It was warm too with the heat from his body. Deep down she could hear the steady throb of his heart. She had never been so close to a man since she had married Mark, and for some reason being close to this man, this stranger whom she wasn't sure she even liked, was much more pleasant than being close to Mark had been.

'The Wilson boys must have heard you. They'd come this way looking for their dog which had run away,' he explained. 'They thought you were the ghost of Emily Greville which the natives believe walks every fifteenth of March, the day she's supposed to have jumped to her death. They told their father what they'd heard and he told me when he came into the bar at the hotel. On my way home I decided to call in at the Wilson home to ask the boys exactly what they'd heard or seen, then I brought them with me to show them there wasn't a ghost.' He gave a grunt of laughter. 'I guess I won't be so quick to disbelieve those lads in future,' he added. His arms slackened their hold about her. 'Are you all right now?' he asked.

'Yes—yes, thank you,' she whispered, leaning

back, suddenly feeling shy of him because he had held her against him and because she had enjoyed being held by him. 'But I still feel a little queer in the head.' She pushed her hair back.

'I expect you're hungry,' he said practically getting to his feet. 'Why don't you lie back and relax while I go and fix you something to eat.'

He walked away from her and disappeared behind a partition on the opposite side of the circular room. Feeling hazily comfortable, having no desire to move, and feeling strangely glad because for once someone had taken over the direction of her life for a while, Lori lay down again and let her gaze drift round the room.

The curving rough stone wall had not been plastered. It glowed in the lamplight. A large cupboard had been built against part of the wall, following the curve. Its doors had been left carelessly open and she could see its shelves were stacked with paper and rolls of canvas. In the middle of the room there was a big easel with a light rigged up over it to shine down on the stretched canvas that was propped against it. A huge table had been pushed to one side of the room and it was cluttered with jars holding brushes, paints and other equipment. Against another part of the circular wall colourful paintings had been stacked.

It was the strangest room she had ever been in, untidy yet colourful, and, obviously a hive of activity, rough yet somehow beautiful, expressive of the man who lived and worked in it. And she felt safe there, safe and comfortable. Her eyelids drooped and she dozed.

CHAPTER THREE

'I HATE to disturb you when you seem to be sleeping so peacefully, but I really think you should eat something.'

Rick spoke near to her and Lori opened her eyes. He was sitting on the edge of the couch again, leaning slightly towards her, and through a haze of drowsiness she saw him as a golden-skinned, tawny-haired, green-eyed god who had condescended to step down from his pedestal for a short time to rescue her and bring her to safety, and she experienced a strong desire to reach out and hug him to show her appreciation of his kindness and help.

Then her eyes focussed properly and she saw him more clearly, as she had seen him before. He was a tough-looking man, and experience of life had carved deep lines across his forehead and down the lean cheeks of his hardbitten sun-weathered face. He had a straight arrogant nose and wide-set eyes as cool and wintry as arctic seas. With his unruly sun-bleached hair and his casual denim shirt unfastened almost to his waist to reveal his broad suntanned, hair-crisped chest, he wasn't the sort of man who attracted her at all. He was too unconventional . . . and yet the desire to hug him persisted, surprising her.

'Can you sit up?' he asked.

Lori nodded and pushed herself up. He went

over to the cluttered table and returned carrying a tray which had four short legs and set it across her knees. On the tray there was a plate of scrambled eggs, some toast and a mug of milky coffee. She gave him a shy upward glance.

'Thank you,' she whispered, and picking up a fork from the tray began to eat.

Rick moved away and she watched where he went. He disappeared behind the partition again and reappeared with another mug of coffee. He came over to the couch and sat down beside her. Leaning back, he sipped coffee while she continued to eat. Silence stretched between them, broken only by the sound of Lori munching toast and the click of her mug against the surface of the wooden tray when she put it down.

'When made you come to Dorada to work for Bernice Alden?' Rick asked in his abrupt way, startling her. She gave him a quick sideways glance. He was watching her.

'I wanted to have a change, do something different,' she replied noncommittally, paused, then added lightly, 'I wanted to see a tropical island.'

'How do you get on with her?' he asked.

'Quite well. She's very bright and knows a lot about the history of the islands. Haven't you met her?'

'No.' His mouth quirked wryly. 'We don't move in the same social circles. Apart from Tracy the Aldens aren't noted for their neighbourliness nor their generosity, and I doubt very much if Mrs Bernice Alden has ever set foot in the places I frequent, such as the hotel at Denny's Beach.'

'I know she hasn't,' replied Lori. 'She told me she doesn't care for such places. She told me also that she thinks you're an adventurer and that your name isn't really Greville. She says the Grevilles were English aristocrats and that there's nothing aristocratic about you,' she added daringly, and watched from under her lashes for his reaction. The ironic twist at the corner of his mouth sharpened and his eyes narrowed unpleasantly.

'Did she now? How snobbish and narrow-minded of her!' he drawled. 'Well, she's wrong in her assumptions about me, your so clever historian. I am a Greville and I inherited this portion of the Greville estate fairly and squarely from my grandfather Robert Greville, who was a direct descendant of the Greville who planted the estate way back in the eighteenth century. And if Grandfather hadn't been pushed for money to pay his debts in England Tamarind would be mine now too. He sold it to the American oil millionaire who owned the property before your pulp and paper friends from Canada took over.'

'The Aldens aren't my friends. In the city we come from they and I don't move in the same social circles,' she retorted with a touch of humour, and felt pleased when she saw his lips curve in a grin of appreciation. 'You don't speak like a person from England.'

'That's because I didn't grow up there, I suppose,' he replied. 'My mother died when I was about five and soon afterwards my father, who was an artist too, left England and took me with him. He was a wanderer and we lived in

many different countries before settling for a
while in Southern California, where I managed to
get some high school education. That's where he
was teaching at art school when he died about
eighteen years ago.' He broke off to frown
morosely at his empty coffee mug.

'Did he teach you how to draw and paint?' Lori
asked.

'He taught me many things—how to draw, how
to paint, how to carve, how to etch. He also taught
me how to live, to make the most of being here on
this earth, to appreciate the beauty not only of
nature but of people.' He paused again, then added
in a low voice. 'God, I was lonely after he died!
Lonely and poverty-stricken and it took me a while
to learn that I had to put myself first if I was going
to survive and achieve my ambition to be a
sculptor. Have you had enough to eat?' he added.

'Yes, thank you. It was good. Do you have a
bathroom?'

'Sure. It's up the stairs.' He indicated a
wrought iron spiral staircase which wound up to
the second floor. 'It's partitioned off from the
bedroom.'

He took the tray from her and she stood up,
relieved to find that her head didn't whirl any
more. She went slowly up the staircase and into
the bedroom. It was another strange room with
inward-sloping stone walls. There was a wide
divan bed, unmade, and a chest of drawers, the
drawers of which had been pushed in carelessly
so that articles of clothing hung out of them. On
the floor by the bed lay a shirt and a pair of faded
paint-spattered jeans. The room was a mess, but

it could be made to look attractive, Lori thought, if it was decorated and looked after.

She went into the small bathroom which was separated from the rest of the room by wooden partitions. It was fairly clean but the one and only towel lay on the floor. She picked the towel up and hung it on its rail, used the lavatory, then washed her hands and face. In the small mirror over the washbasin she noticed her face was extremely pale again and her hair was tangled. Her blouse was streaked with dirt and so was her cotton skirt. Going back to the bedroom, she searched among the collection of items on the dust-laden top of the chest of drawers, found a comb and dragged it through her thick hair.

When she thought she looked neater she turned away and found the unmade bed in her way. Almost before she realised what she was doing she was plumping the pillows and straightening the creased sheets. There was only one blanket, a brightly coloured one, something like an Afghan, and she was smoothing it over the bed when footsteps sounded on the iron stairs. Rick appeared at the top of them.

'I thought you'd passed out again,' he said, then he saw what she was doing and his whole manner changed from one of concern to mockery. 'Well, well, well!' he drawled, stepping over to the bed and facing her across it. 'So you've decided to sleep up here, have you? With me?'

'No!' she exclaimed, colour flaming in her cheeks. 'That isn't ... you mustn't think that because I'm making your bed I want to sleep with you,' she stammered.

'Then why have you made it?' he demanded. Standing with his legs apart, his thumbs hooked in his belt, he stared at her in that cool objective way as if he were studying her closely, trying to penetrate her mind.

'I just can't bear the sight of an unmade bed, I suppose,' she retorted. 'You're very untidy,' she added. 'You should make your bed every morning, soon after you get up, and . . .'

'I like the air to get to it,' he interrupted her.

'At the orphanage we were always taught to make our beds as soon as we'd dressed. And we were never allowed to throw our clothes on the floor like you do.' Lori bent and picked up the shirt and jeans.

'Leave them alone!' he roared at her in the same way he had roared at her to sit still in the airport on Sint Maarten. In a few panther-like strides he was beside her. He snatched the clothes from her and dropped them on the floor again. 'I don't like women who insist on tidying up after me,' he said through his teeth.

'And I don't like men who make disaster areas of the places where they live,' she retorted.

There was a short silence while they glared at each other. Both of them were breathing faster than usual. The smaller, higher room was warmer than the big downstairs studio room and not as brightly lit. Lori felt sweat prick her skin and she saw the sheen of it on Rick's skin at the base of his throat where a pulse beat strongly.

For some reason she couldn't take her glance away from that smooth glistening hollow and an errant and, surprising for her, erotic thought flitted through her mind. What would it be like to stroke his sun-bronzed skin with her fingertips? What would it be like to rub her cheek against his chest or touch that pulsing hollow with her tongue to taste it?

Alarmed by her sudden sensuous reaction to him, Lori gasped for air and backed away from him into the space between the bed and the chest of drawers. She swallowed hard and her hands clenched on the stuff of her skirt.

'An orphan, eh?' he murmured, his finely drawn arching eyebrows tilting mockingly. 'An orphan and lately a widow. No wonder you have a lost look about you! It caught my eye in Sint Maarten. I suppose you're always looking for someone to take care of you; always hoping some guy will come along and want to be your daddy,' he taunted.

'No more than you're always searching for a woman who will mother you, who'll pick up your clothes, make your bed and cook your meals,' she retorted angrily. Her blood seemed to be boiling in her veins and her breasts were heaving beneath the thin cotton stuff of her blouse. 'Oh, I might have known you wouldn't stay kind for long,' she seethed. 'Please will you get out of my way. I'd like to leave now and go back to Tamarind.'

Rick didn't move. The hostile glitter had faded from his eyes and they seemed to have softened and darkened. He wasn't looking at her from a professional artist's point of view now. He was looking at her as if he had one thing in mind; as if he wanted to touch her, kiss her, take her body between his powerful sculptor's hands and mould it against his, leave his imprint on it and in it.

'Please,' she whispered, thoroughly shocked by her own thoughts. 'Please step aside so I can leave and go to Tamarind. Mrs Alden will be wondering where I am. She gave me the afternoon and the evening off, but I didn't tell anyone where I was going. They . . . they might be looking for me.'

'I doubt it,' he drawled. 'And you'd never find your way back in the dark across the fields and through the bush.' He stepped closer to her and she smelt the tantalising scents of his suntanned skin.

'Then I'll go by the road,' she said, feeling the roughness of the stone wall strike through her thin clothing as she came up against it when she stepped back from him again.

'It's about six miles by road,' he replied. 'Too far for you to walk tonight after what you've been through.'

'Could you drive me in your jeep, then?' she croaked.

'I could, but I won't,' he said softly. 'You don't have to go, love. You can stay and lie down on this bed that you've made so neatly and sleep with me and I'll take you back to Tamarind at sunrise. I'm sure you'll be able to slip into the house without anyone seeing you or knowing you've been out all night.'

'No.' She spoke shakily but firmly. But hardly had she denied him that she was suffused by the hot pulsing desire to feel his lips against hers and his hands at her breasts. 'No, I can't stay. I mustn't stay,' she muttered.

'What is it, Lori? What is it you're afraid of?' he asked, frowning at her as if he were puzzled by what she had said. 'Surely you're not afraid of this?'

His face swooped down towards hers. His lips pressed against hers. For a moment she was still, not knowing what to do. Then incredibly something seemed to burst open inside her, like the petals of a flower burst out of their protective sepals when they feel at last the warmth of the sun. Her lips trembled and parted at the soft seductive touch of his and she swayed against him, her eyes closing.

Rick made an exclamation against her mouth and his arms went around her, crushing her slender body against the rock-like hardness of his. Keeping hold of her, he stepped sideways and they both sank down on to the bed until they were lying across it.

There was a drumming in her ears and she felt as if she had dived too deeply into the sea, but for a few minutes she didn't care what happened to her as the longing to be made love to which she had repressed for so long swept over her, obliterating all logical thought. Her lips parted hungrily and she returned his kiss with interest, learning what to do from him. Her fingers found his skin at last and ran riot over his chest, his throat and his cheeks, tangling finally in his hair.

It wasn't until she felt his hand, the fingers hard and muscular, stroking up her thigh, slowly and caressingly, sliding under her skirt, that she panicked and struggled to the surface of the deep dark pool of passion into which she had plunged.

She realised where she was and with whom, and
what they were doing and where it would lead.
Fear was a draught of icy air chilling her. She
pushed free of Rick, scrambled to the side of the
bed, intending to run to the stairs and down; to
escape not just from the touch of his desire but
also from her own newly wakened desire to touch
him.

She was just putting her hands down on the
bed to push herself up when his arm came
around her, hugging her closely about the waist,
his hand curving to her breast. She stiffened
and her hands went to his hand to pull it away
from her.

'Let me go,' she whispered. 'Oh, please let me
go!'

'Tell me why you're afraid,' he murmured, and
his breath wafted the delicate skin at the curve of
her neck, tickling it deliciously.

'I'm not afraid,' she replied as steadily as she
could.

'Yes, you are,' His hand closed more surely
around her breast. 'I can feel your heart beating
too fast. You're frightened of something.'

'No, no I'm not. I . . . I just want to go back to
Tamarind. Please let me go—please!'

Rick slowly withdrew his arm, and immediately
she was on her feet and turning to face him. Half
lying on the bed, one arm supporting him, he
stared at her from under frowning brows.

'We could have fun together, you and I, if
you'd stay the night,' he said softly. 'We could
get to know each other better.'

'I can't stay with you. Oh, don't you see? Mrs

Alden might find out and object. I might lose my job,' she argued.

'Lose your job?' he exclaimed, his eyebrows going up in mocking surprise. 'Oh, come on, Lori, this the second half of the twentieth century and we're two adults, and if we choose to spend the night together it's our business and not your employer's. . . .'

'But I don't choose to stay with you,' she interrupted him stormily. 'It's you who doesn't see. I'm not the sort of woman who stays the night and sleeps with any man who happens to be around. I . . . I'm not a good-time girl like . . . like Tracy Alden, and I'm going back now to Tamarind.'

She whirled away from the bed and ran swiftly down the spiral staircase before she could change her mind. Her head was aching and her legs were shaky, but she kept on going to the door of the mill. She tugged it open and stepped out into the soft warm air of the scented tropical night.

The door closed behind her. By the light shafting out from the windows of the mill she was able to find her way along the path to the narrow road, thence to the coast road, but once she had turned right to walk towards Tamarind, the thick darkness closed in around her, reminding her of the terror she had experienced in the small outhouse. Only the light of the stars twinkling in the blue-black sky, only the sound of the wind rustling the fronds of the palms and the feel of it on her skin, only the sound of the ocean singing on the unseen shore kept her going and stopped her from taking fright at the shapes of bushes looming before her. She did stop once and cry out, her hands going to her face when something soft and furry, she hoped it was a moth, zoomed into her cheek.

Under the thin soles of her sandals the surface of the road was rough and sharp-edged stones pricked through. It seemed a long, long way to the bend where the road turned right to go up the hill, and by the time she reached it her legs were aching and her head was throbbing and she was regretting having left the shelter and easy relaxed atmosphere of Rick's studio.

Supposing she hadn't panicked when she had been lying on the bed with him? Supposing she had allowed passion to overwhelm her and had stayed the night with him, would she have learned with him what ecstasy was like? Would she have experienced sexual fulfilment with him, a stranger whom she had known only a few hours? She hadn't experienced it on her wedding night with Mark whom she had known for almost three years and whom she had loved. Or thought she had loved.

What was love? Once when she had examined her feelings about Mark, when she had got cold feet about marrying him, she had looked up the word in the dictionary to find out if love had been what she had imagined she had felt for him. The definition given had not helped her at all. According to the dictionary love was *warm affection, attachment, liking or fondness for, to, of a person or thing*. The second definition had described love as also being the sexual passion or desire between sweethearts or married couples.

Eventually she had decided that since she had liked Mark she had loved him, and she had gone through with the marriage ceremony only to find on their wedding night she had felt no passion leap up within her when he had kissed and fondled her. She remembered how cold and blank she had felt, how upset because she had been unable to respond. He hadn't seemed to notice and had taken her anyway, forcing himself upon her without any consideration of her needs or feelings, and she had lain awake for the rest of the night, dry-eyed, staring into the darkness while Mark had slept, wondering why she had married him.

But tonight, back there in his bedroom at the sugar mill, she had responded to Rick Greville long before he had ever kissed her, yet he was a man she hardly knew and hadn't even liked at first. Why had she wanted him to kiss and touch her? Why had she wanted to kiss and touch him? What had happened? One minute they had been snarling at one another, the next instant they had been in each other's arms.

Perhaps it was the tropical heat. Lori had heard that the torrid temperatures had an aphrodisiac effect, causing people to want to make love. Yes, that must be it. It couldn't be anything else. It couldn't be love. She couldn't possibly be in love with a man as uninhibited and as disreputable as Rick Greville appeared to be.

But she had liked being in his arms, had responded eagerly to the warmth and generosity of his kisses and felt her body sing with desire when he had touched her. . . .

Behind her she heard the throb of an engine. A vehicle was coming along the road. Tracy, perhaps, returning from some nocturnal spree. Lori put a damper on her erotic thoughts and stood at the side of the road ready to put out her hand and signal for a lift. The twin beams of headlights lit up the road and shone into her eyes. Beyond the shafts of light she could see the gleam of white paint and recognised the vehicle as Rick's jeep. She didn't raise her arm but waited until the jeep stopped beside her.

He braked and the clatter of the engine stopped as he turned off the ignition.

'Get in.' His voice was rough and growling.

'How do I know you'll drive me to Tamarind?' Lori asked hesitantly.

'You don't. You'll just have to take a chance,' he retorted dryly. 'Come on, hop in. You can't walk all the way. Nor can I let you.'

Lori hesitated no longer. She was too tired to refuse his offer of a lift, too tired to resist even if he did turn around and drive back to his studio. With a sigh of surrender she climbed into the jeep and sat down on the hard bench seat beside him, her feelings about him warming up again. He had been concerned about her, so he'd followed her. For that alone she could love him, she thought.

'I still don't know why you backed off when you and I had something good going between us just now,' Rick said softly, turning towards her and resting his arms along the back of the seat behind her. 'Did he ... your husband ... frighten you on your wedding night? Did he hurt you? Is that why you withdrew and ran away from me?'

Shocked as well as surprised by his penetration into her most secret thoughts, Lori sat for a moment in stunned silence. How could he know so much about her after knowing her for only a short time? Then quickly the habit of years took over and she tried to cover up, not wanting him to get too close to her.

'I don't discuss personal matters with strangers,' she said stiffly.

'Don't or won't?' he asked jeeringly, and when she didn't answer he went on even more scornfully, 'I guess Tracy was right when she said you're a puritan. You won't pose for me, you won't go to bed with me and now you won't talk about something you've been bottling up inside you for so long it's inhibited you, repressing your natural instincts. You want to make love with me, but you won't let yourself go. Why?'

'It . . . it's none of your business,' she retorted weakly.

'Is it because we're not married that you won't give?' he demanded, still jeering. 'Would you pose for me, go to bed with me and tell me your secret problems if we were married? Does marriage, to your mind, make nudity, lust and the sharing of problems legal and therefore acceptable?'

'I suppose it does,' she said rather wildly. Her blood was boiling again. Rick had the power to rouse her emotions more than anyone she had ever known. He could make her more angry, more confused than she had ever known she could be.

'Then we'd better get married as soon as we can,' he said tauntingly, 'because I'm going to have you as a model and as a bedmate before this month is over.'

'Oh, stop it, stop it!' she shouted at him. 'You're crazy!' She would have got out of the jeep, but he grasped her arm, his finger curving round it just above the elbow. The touch of his warm hand on her cool flesh had the effect of melting her resistance to him, and she stayed in the jeep.

'I think I must have gone crazy too,' he agreed with her, a strange bitter edge to his voice, 'because I certainly didn't come after you with the intention of proposing to you. Marriage is too restrictive for a creative artist like me.'

'But why me? Why do you want me?' she whispered, trying to lean away from him because she was finding the throbbing heat of his body almost overpowering and had a longing to feel his arms around her again, holding her closely while he kissed her.

'Maybe it's because you keep saying no and I've never been able to take no for an answer,' he said. He stroked back the swathe of hair which lay coiled against her throat. His fingers lingered lightly and sensuously against her skin, sending delicious shivers through her. 'Come and live with me. Leave Tamarind and come and live with me for a while, pose for me, come, be my love. it could turn out to be the best thing that's ever happened to either of us.'

'No, no!' she muttered frantically, much closer to surrender than he would ever know.

'Shush! Don't say that word to me.' Rick's fingers pressed against her lips and above her she saw the dark shape of his head as it tipped towards hers. When he spoke again his breath was warm on her lips. 'This isn't the end of it,' he whispered. 'This is just the beginning, and one day you're going to come and pose for me and live with me.'

'No!' The word came out in a shaky gasp before his lips crushed hers in another sense-rousing kiss.

They were both breathless when it was over and let go of each other with reluctance.

'Going to change your mind and come back to the studio with me now?' Rick asked.

'No.' Now it was hurting her to deny him. 'I can't. I must go back and see Mrs Alden—I must. I owe it to her to tell her where I've been and why I'm so late.'

'And if she throws you out, what then? Will you come to me then?'

'I don't know—I don't know. Oh, I'm all mixed up,' she muttered. 'I'm so tired I can't think any more. Please drive me to Tamarind, *please!*'

Rick didn't say any more. The engine roared and he put it in gear. Tautly Lori sat fully expecting the jeep to turn in the road and go back the way it had come, back to the sugar-mill studio. But it didn't. It climbed up the hill, turned on to the narrow paved road which led to Tamarind and swerved in between the gateposts to stop in front of the house.

Light gleamed yellow inside the house but no

light shone out from the front window and th
lantern-shaped lamp over the door wasn't li
Rick didn't stop the jeep's engine and after
quick glance at him Lori stepped out of th
vehicle on to the path.

'Thank you for ... for rescuing me and fo
bringing me here,' she said, then added firmly
'Goodbye.'

'Not goodbye but *au revoir*,' he retorted
'Because we're going to see each other again. I'l
come for you tomorrow.'

'No!' shouted Lori, but the jeep shot forward
swerved around the round flower bed an
charged out on to the road. It turned sharply an
disappeared, the sound of its engine vibratin
through the air long after it had gone, beating u
from the coast road to Lori, who stood silent an
still in the shadow of the casuarina trees tha
sighed softly in the wind. Only when she couldn'
hear the jeep any longer did she turn at last an
walk to the front door.

To her relief the door opened easily and quiet
when she turned its brass knob. She stepped int
the house and turned to face the door to push
shut as quietly as she could. The latch had jus
clicked home when she was startled by light
going on. Swinging round, she came face to fac
with Tracy.

With her blonde hair glittering like tinsel in th
electric light and her long body swathed in whit
chiffon negligee Tracy looked somewhat like a
angel, but there was nothing angelic or sym
pathetic in her hard pale blue eyes as their glanc
shifted over Lori.

'My God, where have you been? What a mess you're in!' she exclaimed. 'What have you been doing? Rolling in a cane field with some guy, from the looks of it. Do you know it's past four in the morning?'

'I . . . I'm sorry I'm late. . . .'

'Late? Don't you mean early?' scoffed Tracy. 'Save your excuses for Granny Bernice. She's nearly having a heart attack! She's all worked up because she thinks she must have made a mistake bringing you here and giving you a job. She says she wouldn't have offered you a job if she'd known you'd do something like this, but she had the impression you're a nice well-behaved young woman.' Tracy's mocking laugh trilled out. 'It just shows how easily someone like her, more interested in the past than in the present, can be deceived by appearances, doesn't it?' she said mockingly. 'You'd best come to her room now and explain. She won't sleep until she's seen you and given you the third degree. Come on.'

Lori's feet dragged as she followed Tracy up the stairs to Bernice Alden's suite of rooms. She felt drained of all her small resources of energy and she craved sleep; to sleep and sleep for a long time and to find when she wakened that all that had happened to her since she had left Tamarind that afternoon had been a dream.

In the elegantly furnished bedroom with its four-poster canopied bed and Persian scatter rugs Bernice was in bed, propped up by fat, silk-covered pillows. Forgetful of her soiled clothing and tangled hair, Lori hurried to the bedside. To her consternation Bernice looked very frail, her lined face was white and her lips had a strange tint of blue, but the expression in the heavy-lidded hazel eyes was stern rather than reproachful.

'Here she is at last, Granny Bernice,' Tracy sang out. 'And guess who brought her home? Rick Greville! I told you he'd asked her to pose for him, didn't I? I guess that's where she's been all this time, posing in the nude in his studio!'

'I haven't been posing for him.' said Lori hotly, turning to glare at Tracy. 'And I haven't been in his studio all the time.'

'Then where have you been?' Bernice asked, and Lori looked back at her. It was a long time since she had had to account to anyone for her whereabouts during her spare time, and now she felt resentment rising in her because she would have to explain to her employer in front of the mocking, hostile Tracy.

'It's a long story, Mrs Alden,' she said quietly 'And I feel very tired. Perhaps I could tell you in the morning. . . .'

'I want you to tell me now,' insisted Mrs Alden querulously. 'Did that Greville man really bring you back here?'

'Yes, he did, but. . . .'

'Then you have been with him until just now.'

'I was with him for a short time, but. . . .'

'Yet I had made it clear to you, I had thought that we don't associate with him,' said Bernice her voice rising. 'And that means we don't like any of our employees to have anything to do with him. Now did he ask you, as Tracy says she knows he did, to pose for him?'

'Yes, he did—but I refused. And I haven't posed for him,' replied Lori. She was beginning to feel angry.

'You did at Sint Maarten airport,' put in Tracy. Lori flicked a surprised glance at the blonde woman, who was now lounging against the end of the bed.

'I didn't pose for him. He . . . he just sketched me without me knowing it,' Lori explained as patiently as she could. 'Anyway, how do you know he sketched me at Sint Maarten? Did he tell you? You often associate with him. You even invited him to come to the house yesterday.'

'Did I?' Tracy's finely plucked eyebrows went up and she laughed. 'Oh, really! You do like to twist things to suit yourself, don't you? I didn't invite Rick. He came here uninvited, looking for you. I just took him round to the pool where I knew you'd be.' She leaned towards Bernice. 'Honestly, Granny Bernice, I've never invited Rick here, because I know how you and your husband felt about him and because I know Ken's father doesn't approve of him either. No one was more surprised than I was when he turned up here asking if he could see Lori, saying he wanted her to pose for him because he'd discovered she's a perfect model when he'd sketched her at Sint Maarten airport.' She looked at Lori again, her pale eyes sparkling with mockery. 'You'd best come clean, Lori,' she said chidingly. 'I saw you arrive in his jeep fifteen minutes or so ago. How come he brought you back here if you haven't been with him?'

'I . . . have been with him, but only for a short

time, as I've been trying to tell you,' said Lori wearily, turning back to Bernice. 'Oh, please can I go to bed now? I'll tell you what happened tomorrow ... I mean later today ... after I've had some sleep.'

'Did you or did you not go to Rick Greville's studio this afternoon?' asked Bernice.

'No, I didn't. I went for a walk, over the hill. . . .'

'Towards his place,' suggested Tracy.

'Yes, but not to go and visit him. I wanted to see the ruins of the other house. You know that it's fascinated me ever since I came here,' she went on, turning pleadingly towards Bernice again. 'I feel a sort of empathy with the Greville girl who lost her bridegroom on their wedding day,' she added in a whisper.

'Yes, I know that,' said Bernice, nodding. 'Did you go to the house?'

'Yes, but it began to rain, so I stepped into the outhouse to shelter and the wind blew the door shut and I couldn't open it again. I ... I ... was imprisoned there for nine hours. I'd still be there if Rick hadn't come and opened the door. I was very weak, so he carried me to his studio and gave me something to eat and drink. Then he brought me back here.'

'My, my, what an imagination!' Tracy jeered. 'You're in the wrong line of work. You should be writing for one of those true confession magazines. Did you ever hear such a story, Granny Bernice?' Tracy flashed Lori a scornful glance. 'How long did it take you to make it up?'

'I haven't made it up. I'm telling the truth!'

cried Lori. 'Mrs Alden, if you don't believe me ask Rick Greville yourself, tomorrow.'

'He's not coming here again?' queried Bernice.
'I hope not. I really don't want to meet him or to have anything to do with him.'

'And how would we know if he isn't in collusion with you?' demanded Tracy. 'He could even have helped you to concoct your story. What time did you say he found you in the outhouse?'

'I didn't,' replied Lori wearily. Her dream was fast becoming a nightmare in which no one believed what she was saying. 'He said it was about midnight,' she muttered, pushing her hair back from her brow. She was beginning to sway on her feet with exhaustion. 'But there doesn't seem to be much point in telling you, since you're not prepared to believe me,' she added with a touch of acidity.

'Midnight?' exclaimed Bernice. 'And it's now going on for five in the morning! What were you doing all that time? Why didn't you come back here straight away?'

'A good question,' drawled Tracy. 'Why didn't you come back here, Lori, as soon as you got out of the outhouse?'

'I've tried to tell you. I was very weak—there was not much air in the outhouse. I couldn't walk and I was thirsty and hungry. Rick had to carry me.' She spoke in a monotonous tone, too tired now to care whether they believed her or not. 'He was very kind,' she added.

'So he kept you there for four hours and in return for his kindness you posed for him, I guess,' suggested Tracy.

'No, I didn't.'

'Then what did you do?' asked Bernice.

'I rested for a while,' Lori replied, and encountered Tracy's mocking, insinuating glance. Suddenly furious, she blurted out, 'Oh, I know what you're trying to suggest! You're trying to make out that he and I ... that we made love together, aren't you? Well, we didn't. He did suggest I stay the night until I was fully rested, but I insisted on coming back here because I knew you, Mrs Alden, would be worried.'

'Rick Greville kind? Rick Greville behaving like a knight in shining armour and rescuing a damsel in distress?' Tracy scoffed. 'Oh, it's quite unbelievable! Don't you think so too, Granny Bernice, knowing what you do about him?'

'Mrs Alden——' Lori began desperately.

'Enough!' snapped Bernice. 'I've heard enough, and I have to admit that your story does sound incredible, Lori. I'm very disappointed in you. I'd really thought better of you.'

'And I'd really thought better of you!' retorted Lori, coming to the end of her rope. 'And I wish I'd never bothered to tell you the truth. But why should I lie to you?'

'So that you'd still appear to be the nice, quiet, good little girl Bernice believed she had hired,' taunted Tracy. 'That's why. You'd lie to keep your job, of course.'

'If I hadn't wanted to keep my job I wouldn't have come back until breakfast time,' retorted Lori. 'I'd have stayed with Rick all night. And now ... now I'm wishing I had!'

'I think you'd better go,' Tracy said coldly and

authoritatively. 'You're making Granny Bernice feel ill again.'

'Yes, please go, Lori. Please go. Oh, dear I don't seem to be able to get my breath,' gasped Bernice. 'Tracy, please get those pills the doctor prescribed for me. They're in the drawer in the bedside table . . . and some water. I have to take them with water.'

'Mrs Alden, I'm sorry——' Lori started forward, concerned by the rapid change which had come over the older woman, but Tracy stepped between her and the bed.

'Get out,' muttered Tracy through her teeth. 'You've done enough damage. Go on, leave!'

'Leave?' exclaimed Lori. 'But where will I go? I can't leave unless Mrs Alden fires me. She offered me the job, asked me to come out here.'

'All right, all right,' snapped Tracy irritably. 'I didn't mean you should leave the house. Just leave this room and go to bed!'

Tracy swung away to the bedside table and opened the drawer. After glancing anxiously at Bernice, who was lying back against the pillows with her eyes closed and her mouth opened, gasping for breath, Lori left the room reluctantly. Behind her she heard Tracy talking to Bernice, her voice changed and softened beyond recognition as she comforted the older woman.

How the tables had been turned in a few minutes, thought Lori as she walked slowly and wearily along the landing to her room. Instead of Tracy irritating Bernice, she had, and instead of herself soothing and comforting the elderly woman, Tracy was playing the part of a ministering angel.

In her room Lori stripped off her soiled clothing and slipped on her nightgown. After washing and cleaning her teeth she went back to the bedroom, lay down on the bed, put her head on the pillow and closed her eyes.

She wished she hadn't come back. She wished she had stayed with Rick. If she had stayed with him she would have been asleep by now, in his arms. His warmth and his strength would have comforted her. Tears of exhaustion seeped from under her eyelids and slid down her cheeks. Oh, how she wished she had stayed with him!

CHAPTER FOUR

THE morning—or what was left of it—sparkled blue and yellow and green with touches of orange, scarlet and crimson where blossoms blázed on trees and shrubs. The humidity which had made the previous day so sultry had gone and no clouds hovered over Mount Brimstone. Everything was clear and fresh as if newly painted and the trade wind blew steadily.

In the dining room at Tamarind the twin patio windows were open wide as usual. At the table Lori sat eating sliced banana with fresh cream and gazed out at the garden. Around her small yellow birds flitted and twittered. One braver than the others paused for a moment to perch on the edge of the table to stare at her with bright eyes, but when she spoke to it it flew away, swooping out through one of the open windows.

She had slept heavily and had woken late, only half an hour ago, at almost eleven o'clock. She might still have been asleep now if her room hadn't been invaded by Maureen, who had come in, singing at the top of her voice, to clean the room. The small round brown-skinned woman had been surprised to find Lori still in bed and had exclaimed loudly and had rolled her big brown eyes.

'Lordy, what is you doing here, Mrs Stevens?

It's nearly eleven o'clock. Isn't you going to do no work today?'

'Yes, of course I am.' Lori had sat up quickly and then wished she hadn't. Her head had felt heavy and she wished she could have lain down again and gone back to sleep.

'Then you'd best be getting up so I can be cleaning this room,' Maureen had said sternly. 'I'll come back in a few minutes.'

Lori had bathed and dressed hurriedly and gone straight to the kitchen. Lily Carter had eyed her coldly and had told her that Bernice wasn't well and would be staying in bed that day.

'Oh, I'll go and see her,' Lori had said, and had started to leave the kitchen.

'No, you won't,' Lily had said. 'She's asleep right now and no one is to bother her . . . least of all you or Mrs Tracy. Peace and quiet is what Mrs Alden needs, Dr Little says, peace and quiet, and she won't get it if you go rushing into her room.'

'I didn't know the doctor had been to see her,' Lori had replied. 'I didn't know she was feeling so ill.'

'I found her lying on the floor of her room this morning when I went in with her morning cup of tea,' Lily had told her.

'She'd fainted?' Lori had exclaimed.

'She'd had a heart attack,' Lily had announced. 'Lesley helped me get her back into bed and then he went for the doctor. By rights she should be in hospital, but the beds is all taken at the hospital in Williamstown, so the doctor arranged for Sally Harris to come up and nurse her. It's a good thing Mr Clarke is coming today. He'll know what to do, will make arrangements for her.'

'You mean Mr Clarke Alden?' Lori had queried. 'But I thought it was his son who was coming only.'

'They is all coming, Mr Clarke, his wife, Mr Ken and some of their friends. They always come this time of the year for their vacation. You want breakfast now?'

'Yes, please,' Lori had replied. 'But I'll get it myself, just fruit and coffee will do.'

'You is going to have to get it yourself,' Lily had told her rather surlily. ''Cos I is too busy getting ready for the folks who is coming today. From now on until they leave in six weeks' time it's going to be nothing but work, work, work for all of us. A slavedriver, that's what Mr Clarke is.' Lily had chuckled suddenly. 'You hear what I just said? My people was slaves, way back, and here I is still slaving for white folks!'

'But you get paid for your work now,' Lori had pointed out as she had sliced a banana into a dish.

'We get paid, sure, but working for a boss like Mr Clarke Alden is still a sort of slavery. Only when you work for yourself are you really free,' Lily had remarked profoundly.

Lori scooped up the last of the banana and cream and drank the rest of her coffee while she gazed out thoughtfully at the thick luxuriant growth of tropical plants. She had heard back in her home town that the Aldens were considered to be slavedrivers. The thriving multi-million-dollar company was totally in the hands of the sons of Harvey Alden. No one else owned any shares in it, not even Alden wives. Only non-union workers were employed and that way the Alden Company could pay the lowest wages. Working conditions were often poor and when an employee stepped out of line, did something that didn't fit in with the strict moral code of the Aldens, he or she was sacked with a black mark on his or her record, making it difficult to get employment elsewhere. . . .

Lori's eyes went wide and blank. Supposing it happened to her? Supposing she was sacked for being out late last night? Oh, no—Mrs Alden wasn't like that. But Mrs Alden was ill, had had a heart attack. She sprang to her feet and, collecting up the dish and coffee mug, hurried back to the kitchen. The room was full of the smell of freshly-baked bread and Lily was just taking a tray of her golden-brown wholewheat rolls from the oven. At the big scrubbed table Johnson was taking the flesh from the shells of conch which he had probably been diving for that morning.

'Is Mrs Tracy around?' Lori asked Lily after she had washed her dish and mug and was drying them.

'No. She left half an hour ago. She's gone to the airport to meet the boss and his wife,' replied Lily. She looked directly at Lori. 'What you going to do now? You leaving?'

'I . . . don't know. I can't leave yet . . . I haven't been paid for the work I've done.'

'Then I guess you'd best wait until Mr Clarke comes. He'll sort it all out, but there won't be no reason for you to stay here with Mrs Alden sick.

She won't want you to be typing for her when she's in hospital. She won't be writing no history any more,' said Lily. 'You is going to have to look for another job. And you won't get one on this island, I'm telling you now. There aren't enough jobs to go round for our own people, never mind the likes of you. You're going to have to go back to your own country.'

Having no reply to make to Lily's remarks, Lori left the kitchen and went through to the study, closing the door after her. She went straight to her desk and took the cover off the typewriter. If it had been a normal morning she would have typed another twenty pages or so of the history by now. Mrs Alden would have instructed her to do that, she was sure, so that was what she was going to do now ... until someone came and told her that her services were no longer required, and she would have to return to Canada.

She didn't want to go back to her home town. She hadn't been away from it long enough to feel a strong desire to return. But how could she stay in Dorada if the employment situation was as bad as Lily had said it was?

I'd pay you double the going rate for models if you'll come and pose for me. Was it only yesterday that Rick Greville had made his suggestion, had actually offered her a job? Lori felt her pulses leap unexpectedly. It was the first time since she had wakened that she had allowed her thoughts to stray to Rick. She had been afraid to let him enter her mind in case he took over her thoughts entirely. It would be easy to spend the time romancing about him, imagining what it would be like to pose for him, to live with him, and be his love.

Have a torrid affair with a suntanned playboy. Kathy Nolan's remarks returned to taunt her. Rick was certainly suntanned, but was he a playboy? She had always thought playboys were wealthy and idle, but Rick didn't seem to be very wealthy and he couldn't possibly be idle if he was moving up in the art world as Tracy had said he was. Lori didn't know much about art, but she did know that no one achieved recognition for their creativity without hard work and a great amount of self-discipline.

But perhaps in his relationships with women he was a playboy, taking and leaving, giving nothing of himself, making no commitment, and if she did what he had asked last night, if she posed for him, lived with him for a while, became his bed-mate, she might end up being hurt again because she would want more from him than he would be prepared to give. She would want him to love her and her alone in the same way that she would love him.

No, it would be best to avoid involvement with him. Tracy was more suited to have an affair with him and was perhaps already having an affair with him. Tracy would know the rules of the game. Lori frowned as she inserted paper in the typewriter, remembering with puzzlement Tracy's hostility towards her in Bernice's bedroom early that morning. Why had Tracy turned against her?

With a sigh she opened the loose-leaf folder in

which Bernice kept the handwritten first chapter of her history and found the place where she had stopped typing the previous day. Working was the only way to stop thinking about Rick, about Tracy, about Bernice and about her own uncertain future. She read a page through and in a few seconds her fingers were flying over the keys as she typed out what she had read.

She worked steadily for almost an hour and a half, then stopped to read through what she had typed. Vaguely she was aware of people moving about the house, of voices calling outside and other voices answering. She looked at her watch and was surprised to see it was almost one-thirty. She supposed she had missed lunch. Johnson hadn't come as usual to tell her it was ready. But then perhaps he and Lily had forgotten she was there. With the arrival of Clarke Alden, his wife and their guests the Carters would be too busy to remember Mrs Alden senior's helper. Lori's lips curved in a twisted smile. It wouldn't be the first time she had been forgotten in her life. Quiet and not particularly self-assertive, she was used to being ignored and neglected.

The door behind her opened suddenly and she swung round in her chair. A grey-haired man of about medium height came in and shut the door, and looked straight at her with small grey eyes set in a square solid-looking face.

'Mrs Stevens?' he queried.

'Yes,' Lori replied.

'I'm Clarke Alden,' he announced, and walked across the floor towards her, his hands in the side pockets of the jacket of his cream-coloured lightweight suit. 'I believe you came here to work for my stepmother, Bernice Alden.'

'Yes. I've been here nearly two weeks.' Lori rose to her feet. She felt better standing up because he wasn't so very much taller than she was after all, but she didn't like the way his small, mean-looking eyes were staring at her. Nor did she like his pursed-up mouth. 'I'm helping her to write her history of Dorada. . . .'

'You *were* helping her, until this moment,' he interrupted her coldly. 'From now on you're no longer helping her, because she won't be writing any history of Dorada or any other island. I'm arranging for her to be flown to Florida to enter a hospital there, where she'll be under intensive care for a few weeks.'

'Oh, I'm sorry. I didn't know she was so ill,' Lori exclaimed. 'I didn't know she suffered from heart attacks.'

'*She* did, and so did *we*,' he said brusquely, pacing away from her to the window and then back again. 'In fact my wife and I did our best to try and persuade Bernice not to undertake the writing of another history. We also tried to persuade her not to employ anyone to help her with it.' He swung round to frown at her. 'We particularly asked her not to bring anyone out here to work for her. This is our home and we don't want strangers staying here. But she disregarded our wishes—either that or she forgot.' He shrugged his shoulders and his thin lips curled in an unpleasant sneer. 'We've noticed for some time that she's becoming senile.' He gave her a sharp look and snapped, 'You understand what I'm talking about? Sometimes she isn't in her right mind.'

'I understand what you're talking about, but I don't believe Mrs Alden is becoming senile,' retorted Lori, unable to keep her dislike for him hidden any longer. 'And her mind is very clear. She knew what she was doing when she asked me to work for her, and. . . .'

'You really think so?' he queried scornfully. 'I don't, if she'd known what she was doing she would never have asked a potential troublemaker as you seem to be to come and work here.'

'I'm not a troublemaker!' flared Lori defensively. 'What trouble have I caused?'

'It seems that you've been causing Bernice anxiety by associating with one of our more disreputable neighbours ... an artist called Greville. You've been staying at his place overnight.'

'I haven't!' exclaimed Lori.

'Then you deny you were at his studio from midnight last night until about four this morning?'

'No, I don't—I can't, because I was there. But there's an explanation.'

'Oh, yes, there's an explanation,' he jeered. 'And I've heard it—a load of garbage! Tracy was right when she said it sounded like something you'd find in a true confession magazine.'

'If you don't believe it why don't you ask Mr Greville about it?' demanded Lori.

'That's quite enough,' he rapped. 'You've answered back enough, and I have to inform you that in the Alden company we don't care for that sort of behaviour in one of our employees. You're fired as of now. Go and pack your belongings and I'll get Lesley Carter to drive you to the nearest hotel.'

'I'm not leaving until I'm paid,' retorted Lori. 'Mrs Alden hasn't paid me. You can't sack me without paying me for the work I've done first.'

'You're right there,' he acknowledged, taking a wallet from his pocket. 'How much did she say she would pay you?'

'Two hundred and fifty a week, plus my keep.'

'Far too much,' he said nastily, taking several American banknotes from his wallet. 'How long have you been here?'

'A week and four days.'

'Then here's two-fifty American.' He held out the money and she took it. 'Now if you'd just remove your things from the room you've been occupying, which we need for one of our house-guests, I'll tell Carter to be at the front door in about fifteen minutes.'

Turning on his heel, he strode to the door and opened it, indicating with a wave of one hand that she should leave the room. Slowly Lori walked towards the door.

'Your daughter-in-law was wrong, Mr Alden,' she said. 'I didn't spend any nights with Mr Greville. . . .'

'Mrs Stevens, whatever you've done or haven't done during the past week and four days doesn't really concern me,' he interrupted her harshly. 'I just want you out of this house in fifteen minutes. You are not welcome here. Is that clear?'

'But what about Mrs Alden's history? What

shall I do with all the pages of the first chapter
I've typed?'

'That will be taken care of. Now, goodbye,
Mrs Stevens.'

One look at his hard bulldoggish sort of face, at
his small eyes and and thin-lipped mouth, and
Lori saw that there was no point in arguing with
him any more. If she didn't go willingly he would
have her removed forcibly.

'Goodbye, Mr Alden,' she said with as much
dignity as she could, and with her head up, her back
straight, she stepped past him out of the room.

The bedroom she had occupied had been
thoroughly cleaned, she could tell, and the closet
and drawers had been emptied of her clothes,
which had been piled up on the bed. Her two
suitcases were open on the floor ready for
packing, put there presumably by Maureen, who
had been given orders to get the room ready as
far as she could for its next occupant.

Keeping a strict control over her feelings, Lori
put the American dollars away in her wallet and
began to pack quickly. In less than fifteen
minutes she was outside the front door with her
cases at her feet. The blue car swept round the
corner of the house and stopped in front of her.
His brown face impassive, Lesley came and
picked up her cases and put them in the trunk.
Lori opened the car door and sat down in the seat
next to the driver's.

Although she regretted having to leave the
beautiful house she didn't look back at it as the
car went through the gateposts, but she was no
longer able to keep her feelings to herself.

'I'm so sorry Mrs Alden is ill,' she blurted, turning to Lesley.

'So is I, missus,' said Lesley. 'She's a kind lady.' He gave her a sidelong glance. 'You sorry to be leaving Tamarind?'

'Not really. I couldn't stay there now that Mr Alden is there. I . . . I couldn't work for him,' she replied with a shudder.

'What you going to do now, Mrs Stevens?' he asked next, stopping the car at the end of the narrow road and leaning forward to look both ways along the coast road. 'You going to go back to Canada?'

'I suppose so. Could you tell me where I can reserve a seat on the plane to Sint Maarten?'

'You can do that from the hotel,' he replied, steering the car on to the road turning to the left. 'Mr Alden said I was to take you to Denny's Beach Hotel. That all right with you?'

'Yes,' she muttered. 'How often does the plane go to Sint Maarten?'

'Once a day, in the morning.'

'Do you know if I can book flights from Sint Maarten to the mainland from here?'

'You'll have to wait until you get to Sint Maarten to do that,' he replied.

Lori didn't say any more but stared out at the thick green vegetation which edged the roadway, not really seeing it as she faced up to the reality of her situation. She was without a job on an island where jobs were scarce and she had two hundred and fifty dollars. Mrs Alden had provided her with a one-way ticket to Dorada only, so she would have to pay her own way back to Canada.

The air-fare from her home town to the island by way of Montreal and Miami had cost nearly five hundred dollars, she remembered, so to fly back she needed at least another two hundred dollars. And she would have to pay for one night in the hotel on Dorada and perhaps another night in a hotel on Sint Maarten. No, she didn't have enough money to fly back all the way.

'Have you ever been to Canada, Lesley?' she asked.

'Yes, I have. I went to the town of Windsor once, in Ontario. I was working in Detroit at the time on the assembly line at the Ford company,' he replied, surprising her. 'But I didn't like it there, so I saved up my money and I came right back here to Dorada.' He flashed her a grin. 'I didn't like the winters, and I just don't know how you folks up in Canada put up with all that snow and ice.'

'How did you get to Detroit from here?' Lori asked. 'Did you fly?' They were passing the ruins of the old Greville house now and on the hillside behind it Rick's sugar mill glowed, pinkish brown against the lush green vegetation. *And if she throws you out, what then? Will you come to me then?* Rick's softly persuasive words whispered through her mind, tempting her to ask Lesley to drive her up to the mill and leave her there instead of taking her to the hotel.

'No, ma'am.' Lesley's deep lilting voice broke into her wild thoughts. 'I couldn't afford to fly all the way to Detroit, so I went on the Greyhound buses from Miami.' He gave her another sidelong glance. 'Now if shortage of cash is your problem that's the way I'd go to Canada—by bus, from Miami,' he added, guessing accurately at her problem and advising her in a fatherly way, much as he would have advised his daughter or his son.

'Thank you,' Lori replied. The bus—of course! Why hadn't she remembered that she could go all the way from Florida to her home town by long-distance bus through the eastern States, changing at New York or Boston? All she had to do was fly to Miami, and she could afford to do that. She wasn't stranded after all. She could get home if she wanted to.

If she wanted to. But did she want to go home? The ruined house was looming closer. *Will you come to me then? Come, be my love.* The temptation to go to Rick and tell him she had been thrown out of Tamarind was very strong now. The need to see him throbbed in her veins. It was unbelievable, and she had never known anything like it before. She wanted to see him, touch him, feel him, hear his voice either softly mocking her or roaring orders at her. She wanted him more than she had ever wanted anyone or anything in her life. Her hands clenched on her knees, and she opened her lips, licked them ready to speak. The end of the road, the dark ruins flashed by, and the car bumped down the hill towards Denny's Beach.

Lori slumped back in her seat. Sweat was pouring down her cheeks and her heart was beating so hard its noise filled her ears. She groped in her handbag for a Kleenex and wiped her face, glancing sideways at Lesley, wondering if he had noticed how excited she had become.

She was still having difficulty in believing it had happened to her, that she could have been turned on just by thinking about Rick. What was happening to her? What had he done to her?

The road was level now and through the window beside her she could see the surf pounding the long palm-fringed beach. Beyond the sparkling white foam the ocean stretched turquoise blue, glittering brilliantly under the arch of the blue sky. In front of her, through the windshield she could see the hotel looming blue and white amongst its clustering palms and casuarinas. Five minutes later the car slowed down and turned off the road on to a wide gravel path. Lesley stopped the vehicle in the parking lot at the back of the hotel under the shade of some trees.

'You go round to the front, Mrs Stevens, and up the steps, and I'll bring your cases,' he said.

She did as he had told her, walking along a crazy paving path under the deep green shade of close-growing palms. The front of the hotel faced the beach and the singing surf and had a long verandah. Several men were sitting on the verandah at the tables there, most of them seemed to be drinking. The double door leading into the building was open and she went through into a dark cool hallway. She walked over to the reception desk, hearing Lesley bustling in behind her.

'Just you ring that little bell there,' he told her, 'and someone will come. I have to leave you now, ma'am—I have errands to do in Williamstown for Lily.'

'Thank you for all your help,' said Lori,
holding out her hand. 'I'm glad to have met you
and Lily, and Maureen and Johnson.'

'And we're glad to know you, ma'am,' he replied warmly, shaking her hand. 'You take care
now. Watch how you go.'

He went out, and Lori turned back to the desk.
The bell he had referred to was a little old-
fashioned silver handbell. She picked it up and
rang it. Its sound was thin and sweet, and it
didn't sound loud enough to Lori to attract
anyone's attention, so she rang it again more
vigorously.

'Okay, okay, I'se coming, I'se coming!'
grumbled a resonant male voice which sounded
familiar, and she turned round to see Sylvester,
the small thin black man who had spoken to her
at Sint Maarten, come in from the verandah. He
was carrying a tray full of empty glasses. He came
over to the reception desk, set the tray down on it
and then went behind the desk.

'Now what can I do for you, ma'am?' he asked
with a wide friendly grin which seemed to split
his face in two, then immediately recognised her,
his brown eyes opening wide. 'Well, it's the little
lady who was at the airport!' he exclaimed. 'You
remember me, ma'am? Sylvester?'

'Yes, I do. I ... wonder if you have a room
vacant for tonight. A single room.'

'We sure have, ma'am.' His grin faded and he
frowned. 'But I thought you're staying a
Tamarind.'

'I was,' she replied a little stiffly. 'But I've left
I want to fly to Sint Maarten tomorrow

morning,' she added, taking the registration card
he had pushed across the desk to her and picking
up the pen provided. 'I'm told I can make a
reservation from here.'

'That's right, you can. Or can I do it for you.
You're sure you want to leave tomorrow?'

'I can't afford to stay any longer.'

'Now why is you leaving, ma'am?' he persisted.
'Don't you like Dorada?'

'I like it . . . but I don't have a job any more, so
I have to leave.'

'You're not working for Mrs Alden any more,
then?' he seemed to know all about what she'd
been doing.

'No. I was sacked this morning.'

'Now that's too bad, ma'am. Too bad,' he
murmured thoughtfully, looking down at the card
she had filled out. He turned away and took some
keys from the rack behind him. 'I'm going to give
you a room facing the sea,' he said. 'You won't
mind the sound of the surf?'

'I don't think so. Is it safe to swim from the
beach?'

'Not really—only if you're a good swimmer.
But we have a pool on the south side of the
building, and it gets the sun most of the day. You
could swim there. Now, you just follow me
upstairs.'

'But what about making a reservation on
tomorrow's flight to Sint Maarten?' she asked,
following him as he carried her cases towards the
stairs.

'I'll do that for you, ma'am, just as soon as I've
shown you to your room. The telephone don't

always work for strangers,' he said with one of his beguiling grins. 'We start serving dinner at six-thirty ... or we're supposed to. It depends on the cook. Sometimes she's late coming. And tonight the Brimstone Trio is coming to give us music for dancing. We like to have a good time here at Denny's Beach.'

The room on the second floor was long and narrow and had its own bathroom. It was kept cool by the steady trade breeze fanning in through the open window. It wasn't as comfortable or as luxurious as the room she had occupied at Tamarind, but it was neat and clean and it was all she required for one night.

As soon as Sylvester had left she unpacked one of her cases, taking out her swimsuit. All the time she had been on Dorada she hadn't swum in the sea, and she couldn't go back to Canada without taking the chance to swim in the surf. She pulled on the swimsuit quickly, wrapped her beach robe around her and found her flip-flops, then made her way downstairs.

In the hallway Sylvester was behind the small bar mixing drinks.

'You going to the pool, ma'am?' he called out.

'No, to the beach.'

'Then just you be careful of that surf. The undertow is treacherous today with that strong wind, and we don't have a lifeguard keeping watch.'

'I'll be careful,' she promised. 'I'm a good swimmer. Did you book a seat on the plane to Sint Maarten for me?'

'I sure did. It takes off at seven in the morning.

Would you like me to arrange for a taxi to pick you up at about six-fifteen?'

'Yes, please—and thank you,' said Lori.

Outside the hotel the sun was still beating down on the sand, but the shadows of the palms were growing longer, sloping across the beach towards the water. The tide was still high but going out, Lori decided. For a while she walked along firm damp sand listening to the surf rumbling and hissing, enjoying just being there and having the time and freedom to do what she liked.

She had never felt free like this before, she thought, had never been able to please herself. All her life, it seemed to her, she had been pleasing other people; the people who had looked after her in the orphanage; her foster-parents, and then when she had gone to work for him, Mark, and more recently her boss at the museum, and then Bernice Alden.

If only she possessed more money she could have stayed at the hotel a few days longer, indulged in a holiday, the sort of holiday she had never had, swimming, basking in the hot sun, visiting other places on the island, perhaps going for a sail on one of the charter yachts she had seen at the marina in Williamstown.

The beach was long, almost two miles, she estimated, and it was deserted. When she reached a part which was sheltered from the wind and the biggest waves by a small rocky peninsula she took off her beach robe and flip-flops and running into the water dived into the first foaming wave that rushed towards her.

The salt water was tinglingly fresh, sluicing over her skin. For a few moments she was in a green sunlit world of water and then she was through, surfacing in the comparatively calm water between two waves. As the second wave came at her, rising up to tower over her, a wall of purple and green water topped by sparkling foam, she dived again right through it, coming up to warm sunshine to float on her back on the swaying surface and letting herself be carried by the surges of the waves back to shore.

Like a dolphin she played, diving under and over the surf, not noticing that the strength of the wind was increasing steadily and that the surf was crashing into the shore more often, with fewer calm troughs between each wave. Then just as she surfaced from one wave another, bigger wave came roaring at her, overwhelming her before she had time to draw breath, knocking her down to the bottom, smashing her against some hidden jagged rocks before lifting her up again and carrying her forward. Blinded by the stinging water, deafened by its roar, Lori struggled to gain her equilibrium, thrashing about with her arms, only to be tumbled over and over as if she were a lifeless doll, her head spinning, her chest hurting as she began to run out of air, knowing that if she didn't breathe soon she would pass out and drown.

'Well, that was a damn fool thing to do!' said a familiar scornful voice.

She opened her eyes and saw hazily a square-jawed suntanned face above hers, wet sun-bleached hair clinging to a broad lined forehead, sea-green eyes looking at her, sharp with concern. Rick, seeming to be completely naked, his tanned torso glittering with drops of sea-water, was kneeling on the sand, bending over her.

'What happened?' she whispered weakly. A need to touch him surged through her. She had to know if he was really there and that she wasn't experiencing one of those strange hallucinations she had read about somewhere that some people had professed to having experienced after being seriously hurt in an accident. Perhaps she was imagining he was there attending to her half-drowned body after it had been thrown on to the beach by the surf. She raised her hand. It seemed to float out towards Rick. It touched the upper part of his arm. Under a cool film of water his skin felt smooth and warm.

She loved the way his skin felt and she wanted to feel more of it. She raised her other hand to stroke his other shoulder. Her hand slid up behind the strong column of his neck, her fingers pressing urgently against his nape. She longed for him to bend his head and to kiss her as he had kissed her the previous night.

His eyes seemed to glint with a wild green fire. His lips parted and his hands reached greedily for her face, framing it as he collapsed on to the sand beside her, stretching his bare body against hers. Open-mouthed they kissed, entwining closely on the damp shadowed sand, bare skin rubbing against bare skin, hands sliding caressingly over cool curves, fingers tantalising warm hollows.

Leaving her mouth, his lips lingered on her throat, the curve of her shoulder and the swell of her breasts, half revealed by the low cut of her swimsuit. The musky, salty tang of his sea-damp hair filled her nostrils, the taste of it was in her mouth, and the desire to be even closer to him swelled up inside her, spreading through her loins in a hot violent rush.

'No, not here, not now,' he murmured thickly against her cheek, and began to move away from her.

'No, no—please don't go away, please stay with me,' she whispered, winding her arms about him so that he wouldn't move. 'Please stay—I want to be with you. I don't want to die. I don't want to die. Don't go away!'

'I'm not going away, and you're not going to die,' he replied with a little laugh, his hands on her wrists pulling her hands away from him as he knelt up on the sand beside her. 'I have to admit there were a few moments when I thought I'd come too late. Lucky for you Sylvester told me where you were. You were caught by the undertow and were being hurled about. I dived in and managed to get hold of your hair. I dragged you ashore and gave you mouth-to-mouth treatment. It worked, and you're still alive, thank God. You're not drowned and I'm not going away, I'm just going to put my clothes on and then we'll walk back to the hotel. Come on, sit up.'

His cool practicality was bracing after the sudden flaring heat of passion. Lori sat up, but immediately felt sick, the salt water she had swallowed rising within her.

'Oh, I think I'm going to throw up!' she

wailed, her hands clutching at her head; she was ashamed that she would have to give way to such weakness in front of him.

'You can do that without my help, I hope,' he said dryly. 'Go on, be sick. I'll turn my back to you.'

She didn't notice where he went, she was too busy vomiting. After a while the horrible retching stopped and she sat shivering, staring at the sea, surprised to see that dusk was falling fast and that the water was a deep wine-red reflecting the sunset glow that flushed the sky. The surf was no longer creamy white but rose-coloured, sparkling here and there with diamonds.

Her beach robe was dropped on to her shoulders. Strong hands curved about the top of her arms and she was lifted to her feet. Dumbly she turned towards Rick and hid her face against his chest, seeking warmth and comfort. His arms went around her. Beneath her cheek the cotton of his shirt was smoother than his skin had been and she could hear the beat of his heart. It should have been the same as when he had held her last night after he had found her in the outhouse. But it wasn't, because now she knew he could rouse her to passion, to hot delirious desire, and never again would she be able to seek the comfort of his arms without wanting to make love with him.

Abruptly she moved away from him, not wanting him to sense how she felt.

'I'm all right now, thank you.' She spoke as clearly and as coolly as she could, not looking at him as she slid her arms into the sleeves of her robe and wrapped it around her, tying the belt tightly at her waist.

'You're sure?' he queried.

'I'm sure.' She gave him a quick glance and noticed for the first time that he was dressed differently. Gone were the faded denims. In close-fitting white pants and a green cotton shirt moulded sleekly to his muscular chest he was an elegant stranger. Only the unruliness of his hair, clustering damply about his forehead and neck, and the cold green glint of his eyes as their glance flicked over her were familiar. 'You're all dressed up,' she remarked.

His eyebrows tilted in mockery and he glanced down at himself. A slight grin tugged at his mouth as he looked back at her.

'That's because I was hoping to take you out to dinner tonight,' he replied easily. 'I went up to Tamarind to see you, but the cook there told me you'd left and had come to Denny's. So I drove down here, and Sylvester told me he was worried about you swimming in the surf.' A frown darkened his face and his lips were thin. 'Why the hell did you have to go swimming in the surf alone?' he demanded roughly. 'Didn't Sylvester tell you it's dangerous?'

'Yes, he did. But I thought I could manage, and I wanted so much to be able to say I'd been swimming from a beautiful beach on a tropical island when I get back to Canada,' she replied.

'You're going back?' exclaimed Rick, his frown deepening. 'When?'

'I have to leave tomorrow. I'm going on the morning plane to Sint Maarten—Sylvester booked a seat for me. I'm staying the night here, at the hotel.'

He continued to frown at her, then with a muttered and rather startling oath he took hold of her arm and together they began to walk towards the hotel.

Darkness was streaking the pale sky and the sea. The surf thundered and the palms rustled. Stars glimmered overhead and lights twinkled from the hotel. The night air was warm and soft, scented with flowers.

A perfect setting for romance, thought Lori wistfully. In silence they walked, and she knew she would never forget the feel of Rick's hand as it slid caressingly down her bare arm to grasp her hand, the nudge of his arm and hip against hers as they walked close to each other, the soft silkiness of sand beneath her bare feet.

CHAPTER FIVE

PEOPLE were sitting on the hotel verandah, dark shapes at small round tables on which candlelight glimmered. Glasses clinked, voices murmured, someone laughed. As Lori and Rick went up the steps the voices stopped and she guessed heads turned. Someone called out,

'Hi there, Rick! Man, do you move fast! She arrived here only a couple of hours ago and here you are holding her hand already!'

The remarks were followed by soft suggestive male laughter. Offended, her cheeks on fire, Lori tried to pull her hand free of Rick's, but his grasp tightened and striding forward, ignoring the remarks, he pulled her after him through the doorway into the entrance hall.

The place was dimly lit and the small bar in the corner was crowded with hotel guests having their pre-dinner cocktails. Sylvester was behind the bar busy mixing drinks with the help of two young black men, but he took time to come from behind the bar to ask Lori if she was all right. She assured him she was.

'She nearly drowned,' put in Rick tersely. 'Good thing you sent me to look for her.'

Sylvester rolled his big brown eyes and clucked his tongue and managed to look severe.

'Now didn't I warn you, lady, not to go swimming by yourself?' he complained. 'That surf just isn't safe at all. Supposing you'd drowned, it would have looked bad—bad for me, bad for the hotel, bad for Dorada. Now don't you do it again.'

'I won't,' Lori promised. 'I won't, because I won't be here after tonight.'

'And she won't be staying the night here, either,' said Rick curtly. 'You know how it is, Sylvester.'

'I guess I do,' Sylvester replied with a sigh and a shrug. 'All right—you know best. See you later, man. Goodnight, miss.'

He went back behind the bar, and Lori turned to Rick.

'What was all that about?' she demanded. 'Why did you tell him I won't be staying the night here?'

'Because you're not staying the night here, that's why,' he retorted.

'I don't see why I shouldn't,' she said, lifting her chin.

'Look around you. Look at the people who are at the bar and remember there are no locks on the bedroom doors,' he said dryly. 'Then tell me you want to stay here tonight.'

Startled, she glanced over at the bar, at the men who were standing there or sitting on high stools. Some of them were staring at her, actually ogling her, and as she looked one of them began to walk towards her. Taking her arm again, Rick turned her away, urging her towards the stairs.

'It's not a place for a woman like you to be staying in alone,' he said in a low voice. 'And Sylvester knows it as well as I do.'

'But . . . but where will I stay the night? I have to stay somewhere,' she whispered.

'We'll sort that one out while we're having dinner,' he replied. 'Now go and change into something suitable for dining in a good restaurant in Williamstown.' His glance flicked over her and a slight smile curved his lips. 'You have to dress up too—I'm not taking you out to dinner with your hair looking like rat's tails! And when you've changed, pack your cases. What's your room number?'

'Twenty-three.'

'I'll come and get you in about twenty minutes. Be ready.'

Lori glanced back at the bar and then looked up at the hard-bitten, suntanned face above her.

'If this place is . . . is what you say it is, why do you come here?' she asked.

'A good question,' he said with a crooked grin. 'I come to have a drink, to talk to Sylvester, to observe people. You could call it my local pub.' His grin faded and his face grew hard. 'But I wouldn't let any woman I care about stay here, and I'm not going to let you stay here. Are you going to do as I ask? Are you going to change, pack your cases and come with me?'

'Yes,' she whispered, 'I'll come with you.' And turning on her heel, she went up the stairs.

In the small bedroom she made sure she had unpacked and had hung up a dress suitable for dining out, then she hurried into the bathroom and turned on the shower. Both the temperature and the pressure of the water were erratic, but at last all the salt was washed from her hair and skin. Wrapping a towel around her, she plugged in her blow-dryer and with the help of a small stiff-bristled brush arranged her hair into its thick flowing waves while she dried it.

Her dress was a simple enough affair. Made from a mixture of cotton and polyester, it had a small pattern of flowers and leaves printed all over it in varying greens. Its bodice was cut low and straight and was held up by thin straps over her shoulders. Its waistline was belted and its skirt was full, falling to an uneven hem just below her knees. She slipped on white high-heeled sandals and draped a white cardigan about her shoulders.

It wasn't until she looked in the mirror above the chest of drawers to make up her face that the memory of what had happened on the beach between herself and Rick came surging back. Her hand shook as she was applying lipstick and she had to stop and wipe off the smear she had made on her chin with a Kleenex. Wide-eyed, she stared at herself.

What had happened to her when she had come round after nearly being drowned? By touching him, by stroking his skin the way she had, she had more or less importuned him, inviting him to kiss her and showing him by the way she had kissed him that she had wanted more from him than just kisses. And then when he had asserted self-control and had withdrawn she had clung to him unashamedly and had begged him not to leave her.

With a groan she covered her face with her hands. What was he thinking of her? He must be laughing at her, especially if he remembered the way she had behaved last night when she had refused to sleep with him and had refused to agree to stay and live with him. Slowly her hands slid down from her face and she stared at herself again, as if by doing so she could find answers to her questions.

She didn't look any different. Or did she? She leaned closer and was surprised to see that her dark brown eyes had a sparkle in them. Her cheeks glowed with a healthy peach colour and her lips, usually set in a straight line, looked fuller, curving naturally and generously as if about to smile. She did look different. She looked as if she had been touched by desire and had found it to her liking.

Excitement throbbed through her suddenly. She picked up the lipstick and this time her hand didn't shake as she applied it to her lips. Had it come too late, this realisation of what had happened to her? This was, after all, her last night on Dorada, the last time she would be with Rick. What would she do? If he asked her to stay and live with him again should she agree and to hell with the consequences?

There was a sharp knock on the door. Turning away from the mirror, she hurried over to the door and opened it. Rick was there.

'Ready?' he asked.

'Not quite. I haven't finished packing yet. Please come in,' she said.

He stepped inside and closed the door. His glance flashed over her.

'Quite a transformation,' he remarked sardonically. 'Do you need help with the packing?'

'No. I can manage, thank you.'

Within a few minutes they were sitting side by side in the jeep. Rick drove fast away from the hotel, turning off the main coast to drive along a narrow road that twisted through several small villages which clung to the slope of the volcanic mountain. He didn't talk, and Lori was content to sit in silence and savour to the full every moment of being alone with him in the warm rushing darkness, determined to make the most of her last night on Dorada.

At last the road began to dip down towards the other coast. The lights of Williamstown appeared and soon the jeep was roaring along the main street, past the old wooden houses, relics of elegant eighteenth-century architecture, some shabby, paint peeling, window frames sagging, some newly done up, paint shining in the lamplight, windows glowing from light within. Past the old market place they drove, dark and silent in the night, past the quayside and into the western, more modern end of the town.

Rick parked the jeep in a narrow alleyway between two buildings and they walked down to the shore. In contrast to the noisy surf and wind on the other side of the island the bay was calm, the water almost black. Offshore the riding lights on the masts of a few yachts anchored in the bay were reflected in the water and beyond them the shape of a big cruise ship blazed from bow to stern with light.

From the beach wooden steps led up to a wide verandah at the back of an old house. Tables were set there covered with checked tablecloths, silver

and glassware. Candles flickered in glass holders
their golden light gleaming on the faces of the
people who were already dining.

The owner of the restaurant was a short stocky
man with a lot of prematurely grey hair, a smooth
olive-tinted skin and a big-toothed smile. He
greeted Rick warmly, shaking his hand, speaking
English with a strong foreign accent. He showed
them to a table in a corner from where they could
watch the glinting sea and the star-pricked sky,
presented them with menus and asked them if
they would like something to drink. Lori said she
would like white wine, so Rick ordered a bottle
and the owner went away.

'Luigi is from Genoa in Italy and he's a very
fine chef,' Rick told her. 'He came here last year
and opened this restaurant. I hope you like
Italian food.'

'I like some of it,' she replied, opening the
menu. 'Why did he come to Dorada? I thought
only natives could work here.'

'I suppose he came here because like many
other members of our generation he was pushed
out of an overcrowded country and had to find
some place where he could survive doing what
he's good at. You'll find many young Europeans
as well as Americans working in the island, trying
to find a niche for themselves. Foreigners can
usually work here if they can do something a
native can't do. Luigi can provide a fine cuisine
attractive to tourists, and since Dorada is trying
to develop as a holiday resort anyone who can
make the place more attractive is welcome.
Luigi's wife is English. She's about your age.'

'How do you know?' she challenged him. 'You don't know how old I am.'

'I'd say you're about twenty-two or three. Would I be right?'

'Too right,' she said with a sigh and a little grimace. 'I'm twenty-three next month.'

'What date?'

'The tenth.'

'So you're an Aries. I'm a Sagittarian.'

'December?' she queried.

'The seventh.'

'And?'

'And what?' He looked up from the menu in surprise.

'And how old are you?'

'Does it matter?'

'I've told you how old I am. It's only fair that you tell me how old you are.'

'I think I'm thirty-six,' he replied absently.

'Oh, Rick!' she couldn't help laughing, unaware how laughter lit up her face, making her eyes dance with light and her soft lips part, showing her well-shaped even teeth. 'You *think*? Surely you *know*!'

'I'm not always sure of the year I was born,' he replied, smiling at her. 'Anyway, I believe age doesn't matter. It's how you feel about a person that matters, not their age, and I hope you're not going to hold my age against me.'

Before she could think of a suitable reply a young waiter, his brown face looking as if it had been polished, came to the table. He showed a bottle of wine to Rick, who nodded affirmatively. The wine was poured into Rick's glass, he tasted

it, and nodded again. Lori's glass was filled an
the bottle was placed in a silver ice bucket whic
the waiter left on a small table beside them. The
he took their order and went away.

Lori sipped some wine. It was cold, dry an
refreshing. She was beginning to feel full
recovered from almost drowning and the light
humoured conversation with Rick about thei
ages and their birthdays had restored her confi
dence where he was concerned. He believed a
she did that age didn't matter and that feeling
were important.

'You're different.' He spoke abruptly and sh
looked at him. His arms resting on the table
holding the stem of his wine-glass between
finger and thumb, he was staring at her with wha
she called his 'professional artist' expression.

'Different?' she repeated, looking down a
herself, at the smooth golden-brown swell of ski
showing above the straight line of her bodice. 'I
must be because I'm wearing a dress,' sh
suggested shyly.

'I wasn't thinking of the way you're lookin
right now, I was thinking of the way you *are*,
Rick murmured. 'You're different from the othe
times we've been together. At Sint Maarten yo
were all prickly and on guard, protecting yoursel
from the foreign environment in which you foun
yourself; protecting yourself from any strangers
At Tamarind you were nervous, not wanting t
offend your employer in any way, inhibited b
Tracy's remarks. And last night——' he pause
and frowned at his wine glass. 'Last night, yo
were frightened of being made love to by me.'

Her eyelashes fluttered as she looked down astily, avoiding his sudden upward glance at er.

'Do you spend your time staring at people, ying to guess what's going on in their minds?' he asked evasively.

'I spend my time observing people as part of y work as an artist,' he retorted coolly. 'And m not guessing that you're different from the ay you've been the other times we've met. You re different. In spite of being sacked from your b, in spite of nearly drowning this afternoon, ou're more relaxed.' He gave her another enetrating stare, his eyes narrowing between eir bronze-coloured lashes. 'You seem almost appy,' he said.

That's because I'm with you. The answer apt into her mind uncontrollably, startling er. Immediately she repressed it. She drank ore wine, set the glass down and fidgeted with

'It's because I'm free for a while,' she xplained hurriedly, not looking at him. 'But I ish I hadn't nearly drowned. I was enjoying vimming in the surf. Now I'll never do it again, ecause of what nearly happened.'

'In the same way you'll never let yourself make ve with a man because of what happened on ur wedding night?' Rick said suggestively, king the bottle of wine from the bucket and filling their glasses. 'Once bitten, twice shy? Is at your motto, Lori, now? Is that how you're oing to go through the rest of your life, unloved d unloving, just because the man you chose to

marry didn't come up to your expectations
bed?'

'How do you know he didn't?' The words we
blurted out of her before she realised what sl
was going to say. She choked back the rest ar
glared back at him, but he grinned cheekily
her. 'I told you last night I don't want to ta
about it,' she replied stiffly, and his grin widen
into a laugh.

'What was his name?' he asked.

'Mark.'

'And what did he do for a living?'

'He was an accountant in the firm
accountants where I worked as a secretary
receptionist.'

'And I bet he was as neat and conventional :
you are,' he jibed, and shook his head. 'He wasn
the type for you, my love,' he added outrageousl
'You need a man who can rouse you.'

'Like you, I suppose,' she retorted tartly.

'Like me,' he agreed equably. 'So you're happ
because you're free for a while. Free from what

'Free from working for someone else,' she sai

The waiter came back carrying a basket
thick wedges of crusty Italian bread, a plate
butter and the endive salad they had both ordere
for their *anti-pasto*. He set everything down ar
departed.

For a few moments they ate in silence. Mus
played softly from hidden speakers. People
other tables talked and laughed. The air w
tangy with the smell of the sea. Candlelig
glimmered on Rick's face, giving it a bronze
look, emphasising the strong moulding of nos

eekbones and jaw. His eyes were hidden by
eir heavy lids while he concentrated on
uttering bread.

He could stare at her and could guess fairly
ccurately at her state of mind because he was a
ained observer and possibly because he was
lder and much more experienced, but Lori
uld go on looking at him and would never
ow what his thoughts or his feelings were.
ly by what he said and did when he was with
r could she judge him. And her judgments of
m were changing all the time as she became
ore and more emotionally involved with him.

He looked up suddenly right at her, his mouth —
nted in its mocking grin.

'Now you're doing the staring,' he scoffed, and
e looked down hastily at her food. 'Are you
ing to tell me what happened at Tamarind and
hy you were sacked today? Was it because you
re out most of last night?'

'Partly,' she replied, relieved that he hadn't
ked her why she had been staring at him.
racy was waiting for me when I went in. She'd
en the jeep and knew you'd brought me back to
e house.'

'So?' His eyebrows lifted. The expression in
s eyes was sharp. 'How did she react?'

'She wasn't very pleasant and she insisted I go
aight to Mrs Alden and tell her where I'd been
d why I was late. She said Bernice had been
rried about me and had almost had a heart
ack.'

'Had she?'

'Not then, but she was in bed, of course, and

didn't look very well. I had to tell her abo
being locked in the outhouse in front of Trac
who made fun of me and said what I'd told the
was like a true confession story. She'd alrea
told Mrs Alden that you'd asked me to pose f
you, and she suggested that was what I'd be
doing all afternoon and that later . . . you'd . . .
mean *we* had been making love until you took m
back to Tamarind.'

'Did Mrs Alden believe Tracy or you?'

'She seemed confused and was too tired to s
anything. She lost her breath and Tracy order
me out of the room. Then this morning when
woke up I was told that Mrs Alden had had
severe heart attack and I wasn't allowed to s
her.'

'Then who gave you the sack? Tracy?'

'No. Clarke Alden.'

'He's at Tamarind?' Rick frowned at he
'When did he arrive?'

'On this morning's flight. His wife has com
with him and they've brought guests to stay. F
told me I wouldn't be needed any more becau
he'd arranged for Bernice to be flown to Flori
to a hospital there. He also told me he hadn
wanted her to employ me. He said she's seni
and didn't know what she was doing when sl
asked me to come out to Dorada to work for he.
Lori's voice shook a little as her feelings abo
Bernice Alden rose to the surface and had to l
expressed. 'But she isn't senile,' she insiste
leaning urgently across the table towards hii
'She's as bright as a button and she's a dear, fii
lady, and I'm so afraid Clarke Alden is going

use this heart attack to put her away in a home for old people where she'll be forgotten and neglected, where she'll rot away. . . .'

She broke off as her emotion got the better of her and had to search in her handbag for a handkerchief. Across the table Rick watched her, a half mocking, half affectionate smile curving his lips.

'Soft-hearted wench, aren't you?' he jeered softly. 'Did Clarke pay you?'

'He gave me two hundred and fifty American dollars. He said that was all he had on him in cash and he didn't want to give me a cheque.'

'Bloody skinflint!' he growled. 'I suppose that's all the money you've got?'

'Yes, but I think it's enough to cover my journey home. I'll fly to Miami from Sint Maarten. From there I can go by long-distance bus to my home town.'

'Not if I can help it,' Rick announced in a hard crisp voice. 'You're staying on Dorada until I've made at least fifty drawings of you in different positions, and possibly a couple of quick paintings too.'

The waiter appeared again, so Lori bit back the quick retort that sprang to her lips. He removed their empty plates and put before them the main course, grilled local seafood served with *pesto*, a strong sauce made from garlic, olive oil, basil and goat's cheese, which Rick told her was a Genovese speciality. Another bottle of white wine was produced and the clear sparkling liquid was poured into their glasses before the waiter left them. For a few moments they ate and drank in silence.

'Did Ken Alden come with his father?' Rick asked casually.

'I think so. I didn't see him. I didn't see any of them except Clarke. Tracy had told him about . . . about last night. He seemed to have believed everything she'd told him and he was very unpleasant about it. Have you ever met him?'

'Once, soon after I moved into the mill. He came over and ordered me to get out,' Rick said curtly. 'He accused me of being a squatter and of having no right to live there.'

'What did you do?'

'I told him to get lost.' The slightly malicious grin slanted his lips again. 'He retreated in disorder, and I heard later that he went to the local land offices in Williamstown to tell them I had no right to be on Greville land and that I was an impostor.' He laughed softly, his eyes dancing with devilry. 'I'd like to have been there to see his face when he was told that the sugar mill and the land around it are mine by right of inheritance!' His face hardened. 'I've no time for slavedrivers like he is.'

'Yet your ancestors who used to live at Tamarind owned slaves,' she reminded him.

'Robert Greville was one of the first plantation owners to free his slaves,' he retorted. 'And what I mean is that I don't like present-day millionaire industrialists like the Aldens who pay poor wages to their employees and refuse to share profits. In fact the less I have to do with any of the Aldens the better,' he added. 'They're not my sort of people.'

'But you seem to be very friendly with Tracy?'

He gave her a scornful look, his long lips twisting cynically.

'You've got it the wrong way round,' he said coldly. 'Tracy is ... or rather tries to be ... friendly with me. She's nothing but a tramp, and now she's scared to death her husband has found out about her recent behaviour on the island and is going to divorce her. Someone must have told him she was having an affair with me.' The green eyes were like chips of ice. 'I suspect your ex-employer, Mrs Bernice Alden. Would I be right? Has she ever said anything to you about Tracy and me?'

'Yes,' Lori admittedly reluctantly. She probed the food on her plate with her fork, frowning a little as she considered Tracy's change of attitude towards herself and towards Bernice the previous night. 'Mrs Alden told me the first day I arrived that Tracy had attached herself to you,' she added. 'She called you "a disreputable artist" '.

His grin flashed out, self-mocking, then was gone, leaving his face harder than ever.

'Attached is a polite way of putting it,' he said tautly. 'I've had difficulty in shaking her off. She's clung like a leech.'

'Then you and she haven't had an affair?'

'No, we haven't had an affair,' he repeated dryly. 'If I'm going to have an affair with a woman I like to be the one who does the hunting and the persuading.' He leaned towards her across the table, his eyes softening as their glance drifted over her face. 'Also I have to be attracted by the woman on more than one level,' he murmured. 'And there's nothing in Tracy to attract me. She's a scheming, shallow bitch.'

'I feel sorry for her,' said Lori. 'She's really most unhappy being married to Ken Alden.'

'She has only herself to blame. She married him for money and nothing else. That's why she doesn't want to give him reason to divorce her, why she's trying to cover up her behaviour now he's come here.'

'She was pleasant and friendly to me at first,' Lori went on, still trying to sort out her thoughts concerning Tracy. 'That's why I can't understand why she turned against me last night, why she made me look bad in front of Bernice and why she told her father-in-law this morning that . . . that I spent the night with you. Do you think . . .?' She broke off to look at him. Rick returned her glance with a wry twist of his mouth and a sardonic glint in his eyes and nodded.

'You've got it. She used you as part of the cover-up,' he drawled. He looked down at his wine-glass which was almost empty and the twist to his mouth increased. 'I expect she was a little jealous of you too because she knew you'd been with me at the mill, a place she'd never been invited to. You'd been able to tread where she'd never been allowed to go, plus I'd asked you to pose for me, something she's been angling to do for some weeks.' He looked across at her again. 'Speaking for myself, I'm glad she had the wits to use your brief association with me to divert her husband's attention from me. I've no wish to be cited as the other man in any divorce suit he cares to bring against her, but I'm sorry it's hurt you and cost you your job.' He tossed off the remains of the wine in his glass and set it down. 'Do you have to go back to Canada right now?' he asked.

'Where else can I go?'

'You could stay here.'

'But I don't have enough money to stay here any longer and the only work I can do is secretarial and I'm sure there are native Doradians who can do that so I'd never get a job.'

'You can work for me. I offered you a job yesterday that no native Doradian can do,' he replied. 'The offer is still open. In fact that's why I went up to Tamarind this afternoon, to invite you out to dinner. I was intending to put the pressure on and persuade you to pose for me. I'm still hoping to persuade you.'

'I know nothing about posing,' she said.

'You'll soon learn, starting tomorrow morning.'

'But I'm leaving for Sint Maarten tomorrow morning,' she argued weakly.

'No, you're not. While you were changing at the hotel I cancelled the reservation Sylvester had made for you.'

'Oh.' Her fork clattered as she dropped it on her plate. 'You had no right to do that,' she said, her voice rising so that the people at the next table turned to look at her. Leaning forward, she added in a loud whisper, 'You have no right to organise my life, no right at all.'

'I think I have,' he replied with maddening serenity as he poured more wine into their glasses. 'You owe me your life. Twice I've rescued you—once from slow suffocation in a dark airless outhouse. . . .'

'You wouldn't have known I was there if those boys hadn't told you,' she interrupted him furiously. 'If I owe my life to anyone it's to them.'

'And I rescued you from drowning this afternoon,' Rick went on aggravatingly.

'But you wouldn't have known I was caught in the undertow if Sylvester hadn't told you I was swimming in the surf, and. . . .'

'*And* ever since then I've been wondering how you've managed to survive for so long without me around to rescue you from your own foolish actions,' he finished tormentingly.

'I've managed very well,' Lori retorted, tilting her chin.

'You've managed, admittedly, but not very well,' he drawled dryly. 'And now you owe me your life, so I'm going to organise it for you.' He leaned towards her and spoke crisply, autocratically. 'You're going to stay a while longer and you're going to pose for me. You'll only have to sit in the mornings, say from nine until noon, and after that the rest of the days would be your own, to do as you like. Think of it as a paid holiday.'

'For how long?' she faltered, strongly tempted by now to do what he asked.

'For as long as it takes me to do enough drawings of you.'

'But I . . . I might not be any good . . . as a model, I mean,' she protested.

'Still worried about the morality of posing in the nude?' he queried.

'I suppose I am,' she muttered.

'Yet there's nothing immoral about it,' he argued. 'Women and men pose in the nude all the time for art students and professional artists. To drew the human figure from a live model is part of the basic training of artists, something all of them have to do, an exercise they have to do continually if they're to retain their ability to draw and appreciate form. There's nothing immoral about it unless either the artist or the model is immoral by nature. Are you immoral?'

'Of course I'm not!' she retorted indignantly.

'So you're implying that I am.'

'No, I'm not.'

'Yes, you are. You're implying that I've taken advantage of every female model who's sat for me.' He laughed suddenly, a crack of ribald laughter that drew attention to their corner. 'My God, if I had, I wouldn't be in such good health today,' he added. 'Who do you think I am? Superman?'

'I didn't imply that . . . that you're immoral at all,' she retorted in a fierce embarrassed whisper. 'How can you say such things? I wish you wouldn't keep on about it.'

'You look very pretty when you're outraged, all pink cheeks and flashing eyes. I must try to outrage you more often. The results are so attractive,' he mocked. 'But whether you intended to imply it or not, you have implied that I won't be able to keep my hands off you if you sit for me without your clothes on,' he taunted wickedly. 'So I'm going to prove to you in the next few days that my original interest in your body was and still is purely artistic. I want to draw it because I want to sculpt it for a project I have in mind.'

'But last night you said ... you said you wanted me to sleep with you,' she said, casting a wary glance at the next table. 'Oh, can't we talk about this some place else?' she whispered.

'We could, but we haven't had dessert yet. Last night, things got a little out of hand, I admit.' Rick smiled slightly, mysteriously. 'I had to find out why you were frightened of me.' He looked up at her suddenly, the smile gone, the expression in his eyes serious, almost sad. 'And I did.' He paused, then added quietly, 'Come and pose for me, Lori, and I give you my word that nothing will happen between us on a physical level unless it's mutual, unless we both want it. And when I've finished the drawings you'll be so many dollars better off than you are now and you'll be free to leave whenever you wish.'

Lori drank some more wine. It flowed through her, easing tension, relaxing inhibitions. Looking at Rick, she saw him again as she had seen him before, through a golden haze, transformed from a tough adventurer marked and battered by experience of life into a golden-skinned, green-eyed, godlike hero who had rescued her twice and who had roused her to desire with his kisses and the touch of his hands. Once again he had asked her to stay with him, and now there was nothing to stop her. She was free to do what she wanted; free to love him, if she wanted to.

She became aware that the waiter had returned and was removing their empty plates. He asked them what they would like for dessert. Lori chose strawberries and cream, but Rick ordered only coffee, and the waiter went away. Across the table they looked at each other.

'You're going to stay, aren't you?' Rick murmured. 'You want to stay.'

He had guessed accurately, as always, at how she felt. She did want to stay a little longer on this beautiful tropical island. She thought of what returning home would be like, the grey slushy streets; the cold biting wind. She thought of what it would be like looking for another job, going for interviews with blank-eyed, hard-faced men or equally blank-eyed, hard-faced women. She thought of Kathy and how her friend would ridicule her for being chicken and for running away from an affair with a suntanned playboy in a tropical paradise. She didn't want to go back home yet, but she was still hesitant, still afraid that if she stayed she might be hurt by Rick.

'Couldn't I stay on a trial basis?' she added diffidently.

'What do you mean?'

'Suppose I stay with you and pose for you for two days, tomorrow and the day afterwards, and if you find I'm no good ... as a model, I mean ... you would tell me and I'd leave, go back home. And if I find I don't like posing for you, if I'm uncomfortable still, I'll tell you and you must promise to let me go. Would you agree to that sort of arrangement.'

Rick stared at her, his eyes narrow and hard as he frowned. Slowly his long firm lips slanted in a rather cynical smile.

'Like most women, you can drive a hard

bargain when it suits you, can't you?' he jeered. 'Two days, when I need you around for at least two weeks!' He picked up his glass and drank the rest of his wine. 'Okay,' he said, setting down the glass and staring at it morosely. 'Two days' trial it is. Two days will be better than nothing, and I agree because I've got to have those drawings of you and we'll assess the situation the day after tomorrow.' He rose to his feet. 'Excuse me, I've just seen someone walk in whom I haven't seen for a long time, and I'd like to have a few words with him.'

He strode away between the tables and through the wide open French windows of the room behind the verandah where there were more tables. Lori watched him go rather uneasily. He hadn't seemed to like her suggestion of a two-day trial, and she wondered why. But she had had to assert her independence somehow, she thought. She couldn't have him thinking he could take over her life just because he had rescued her twice.

'Hello. I'm Joan Bianco,' said a soft English voice, and Lori looked up to see a small fair-skinned woman standing at the table. She had long brown hair tied back from her face with a ribbon and was carrying a tray on which there was a dish of strawberries and cream and a cup of coffee. She set the tray down on the table, put the strawberries in front of Lori and then slid into the chair Rick had vacated. 'Luigi told me that Rick had brought a friend from Canada to dine, so I decided to serve the dessert myself so I could meet you. I met Rick on his way into the other room. He seemed angry about something.' Joan's shining grey eyes considered Lori curiously. 'Do you know why?'

'I think it was something I said to him,' Lori replied cautiously. 'I'm Lori Stevens.'

'Pleased to meet you, Lori,' said Joan, smiling. 'What did you say to him?'

'I told him I'd agree to sit as a model for him on a trial basis for two days. You see, I've never posed before and—well, I'm not sure I'll like doing it or that I'll be any good at it. I thought he'd be pleased when I said I would try, not angry,' she added ruefully.

'I'd have thought so too. I know he's been looking for a suitable model for some time and I would have offered to pose for him, only I knew Luigi wouldn't have approved,' said Joan. 'I used to model to earn a little cash when I was studying at an art college in England. It's awfully hard work, you know, and very boring sitting or standing still for hours on end.'

'Are you an artist?'

'Teacher of art, really. I met Luigi when I went to Italy on an art-oriented tour with the school I was teaching at. And here I am now, a happily married wife and mother. How long have you been here, Lori?'

'Nearly two weeks.' Lori began to eat the strawberries. The ripe fresh fruit burst against her palate, acid-sweet and juicy. The cream was smooth and rich.

'Did you come for a holiday?' asked Joan.

'No. I came to work for Mrs Bernice Alden at Tamarind, but today she was taken ill and I was fired.'

'Oh, what a shame!' said Joan consolingly. 'But Rick came to your rescue,' she went on brightly, 'and offered you a job. He's like that, always helping people. I don't know what Luigi and I would have done without him when we came here last year. Everything went wrong. We were due to open the restaurant at the beginning of December, but nothing was ready. The Italian furnishing, the tiles for the floors and the pictures for the walls we'd arranged to have sent over from Genoa never arrived.' Joan interrupted her breathless narrative to laugh a little. 'We found out later they'd been sent somewhere in Africa! They still haven't come.'

'What did you do?' asked Lori.

'Me?' exclaimed Joan, her finely plucked eyebrows flying up. 'I couldn't do anything—I was like this.' She mimed a rounded shape in front of her stomach. 'I was in the ninth month of my pregnancy, waddling about like an overfed duck and not much use to anyone. If it hadn't been for Rick I think Luigi would have given up and gone straight back to Genoa. But Rick calmed him down and spent a whole week working night and day painting Italian scenes on the walls of the entrance hall, the bar and the inside dining room to create the right atmosphere. He persuaded the local tradesmen to work overtime to fix the kitchen and he found some young men and women to come and work for us as waiters and helpers. And as if that wasn't enough, when the baby started to come he drove me to the hospital and stayed with me until it was born.' Joan laughed again and shook her head.

'Luigi was too worked up to do his duty as a husband and father!'

'Did the restaurant open on time?'

'Not quite. We were a few days late.' Joan looked over her shoulder at the entrance to the other dining room. 'Rick doesn't seem to be in a hurry to come back, does he?' She looked across at Lori again. 'Tell me where and how you met him.'

Lori told her about the meeting at Sint Maarten and then the subsequent meetings on Dorada, leaving out the parts about the rescues and not mentioning Tracy Alden at all.

'Well, I hope your trial period as a model is successful, so you can stay a bit longer on Dorada,' said Joan. 'Don't take too much notice of Rick's moods. He is an artist, after all, and a very good one, so he's entitled to be temperamental.' She rolled her eyes comically. 'Artists and chefs,' she sighed. 'They're all alike, up one minute, down the next.' She gave Lori another inquisitive glance. 'If you've only just met Rick you won't know much about him,' she suggested.

'I know very little,' Lori admitted.

'He hasn't had it easy, by any means. He told Luigi he was so poor after his father died that he had to take all sorts of tough labouring jobs, working on oil rigs and that sort of thing, to earn enough money to pay for lessons in sculpture. He studied in Mexico with Pablo Cosada, for a few years, and married Cosada's only daughter.'

'Oh, really?' said Lori blankly. 'How do you know?'

'I read about it in an article in an American art

magazine I picked up at the secondhand book store we have here where we all trade in books and magazines, circulate them round the island. The article had been written after Rick's first exhibition in the States a few years ago. Where are you going to stay while you're posing for him?'

'He said something about me living at the sugar mill,' mumbled Lori. 'But I'm not sure. I might find somewhere else to stay.'

'Well, it's been nice talking to you,' said Joan lightly, rising to her feet. Rick was coming back to the table. She turned to him and said, 'Would you like to have an after-dinner drink with your coffee, Rick? On the house?'

'No, thanks,' he replied. His glance went from Joan's face to Lori's and he frowned. 'I guess you've been having a good gossip,' he said, turning back to Joan.

'Just making myself known to Lori and filling her in on a few things, that's all,' Joan retorted sweetly, smiling at him.

'You can tell the waiter to bring the bill,' Rick said curtly. 'It's time we were leaving.'

'I will,' said Joan, and winked at Lori. 'Don't forget now, call in to see me any time you're in Williamstown.'

She went away. The young waiter came with the bill, Rick paid it and gave the boy a tip. They left by way of the steps down to the beach and walked in silence to the jeep.

'I think it would be better if I don't live at your mill while I'm posing for you,' Lori said jerkily, breaking the silence as the jeep trundled through the centre of the town past the town hall square with its straggly palms and unweeded flower beds. 'I'd like to stay somewhere else.'

'Where?'

'There must be other better hotels than Denny's.'

'There are, mostly old plantation houses which have been turned into exclusive private hotels for the very rich,' he said coolly. 'A room in one of them would cost far more than you can afford. Also I don't want to waste valuable time driving to pick you up to take you to the studio and then back again. What's wrong with you staying with me at the mill?'

'People will think we're ... we're living together,' she muttered.

Rick swore rather viciously as he changed gear to turn on to the hillside road.

'Are you still worried about appearances?' he jeered. 'Well, I'm not. Let people think what they like.' He paused, then said more quietly, almost soothingly, 'Don't worry about it. You'll have the bedroom all to yourself and I'll sleep on the couch downstairs.' Dryness edged his voice. 'But I'm warning you—I'll want you up early in the morning. Since there's a possibility you might decide you don't like posing and you'll want to leave after two days I'm going to make you sit longer—four hours instead of three in the morning and maybe a couple in the evening too.'

Silence again, heavy and thick, between them. All the lightness she had felt, the near-happiness had gone, driven out by what Joan had told her. No longer could she savour being close to Rick in the warm velvety darkness. Now there was an invisible barrier between them. If she had been a different person, less reserved, she might have tried to break through the barrier by telling him she knew he was married and by asking him why his wife wasn't in Dorada with him.

But she couldn't bring herself to speak to him. She could only hold herself aloof from him, at the same time sensing a coolness in him, a definite withdrawal from contact with her which had begun as soon as she had said she would pose for him on a trial basis. It was as if, having got some sort of commitment from her, he no longer found it necessary to put pressure on her, and she had to admit reluctantly that already she missed his interest and attention.

CHAPTER SIX

LORI flexed the toes of her right foot experimentally. She was lying on a foam rubber mattress which was covered with a piece of dark green material and heaped with cushions. The mattress was on a low roughly made wooden dais. On one side of the dais stood a tall steel pole to which were attached two powerful lamps which could be moved up or down the pole and swung in different directions. The light from the lamps shone down on her body, accentuating curves and hollows with subtle bluish shadows. She lay with one elbow resting on a plump cushion and her right hand supporting her head. Her legs were slightly bent one in front of the other. Before her on another smaller cushion was an open book which she was supposed to be reading.

It was almost noon on the second day that she had posed for Rick, and the interior of the sugar mill studio had been artificially darkened by blinds which had been pulled down over the windows. The atmosphere was becoming stuffy and sweat was beginning to shine on Lori's bare skin. She hoped that soon the bell on the timer Rick had set would ping and the twenty minutes—the longest he would allow her to stay in one position without moving—would be over. Then she would be able to get up and walk about to get rid of the cramp which was jabbing excruciatingly through the muscle of her right leg.

She couldn't see Rick because he was behind her, standing at the big easel painting on a wide canvas, but she knew how he looked. He would be naked to the waist, having stripped his shirt off as the studio grew warmer, and would be wearing only rather ragged cut-off jean shorts. His feet would be bare and his unruly hair would be confined by a sweatband worn about his head. His suntanned face would be set in disciplined lines and the expression in his green eyes would be sharply observant as he studied her form intently before putting a brush-stroke of paint on the canvas.

Yesterday, the first day of the two-day trial, she had almost failed to live up to her promise to pose for him. He had wakened her early, bringing breakfast to her on a tray, cereal and fresh fruit and strong dark coffee, and had told her to be in the studio wearing only a dressing robe as soon as she had eaten and had washed. He had given his orders brusquely and had departed. Still troubled by his coolness, Lori had eaten the food and then had reluctantly left the bedroom to go down to the studio where he had been arranging the lamps around the dais.

'I'm going to spend this morning doing many quick sketches of you in various positions,' he had said. 'Now I want you to behave as naturally as possible. Think of the couch as a bed, if you like, and move about as you would normally when you first wake up in the morning, stretching, sitting up, getting off the bed, walking to the closet, taking out an article of clothing. Use your imagination. Now get up on the dais and take your robe off.'

With her hands on the tie belt of her robe she had watched him perch on a high stool at the easel. A drawing board had been resting against the easel, and to it Rick had clipped several sheets of rough paper. He had looked across at her.

'Go on—move!' he had ordered sharply. 'Get up on the dais and take your robe off.'

'I . . . I can't do it. I'm sorry, I can't do it,' she had muttered, and had started to hurry over to the spiral staircase. He had sworn, one sharp word, and had slid off the stool to step in front of her.

'You promised to stay for two days,' he had snapped at her. 'And you're going to do it. Now turn your back to me, pretend I'm not here, walk up on to the dais and take your robe off.'

Lori had stood her ground for a few moments, staring up at him, defying him, thinking of dodging around him and making a run for the stairs.

'Don't do it, Lori,' he had whispered, his lips taut. 'I've only to put out an arm and I'd catch you, and if I have to touch you, you know what will happen. Don't put my self-control through too stiff a test. It might snap, and then you'd hate me and would have every good reason for refusing to pose for me.'

Still staring at him, she had stepped back, away from him. Turning, he had walked back to the easel. Out of the corners of her eyes Lori had watched him perch on the stool again. He had leaned forward to adjust something and his face had been hidden by the drawing board. In that moment she could have rushed towards the stairs again. She had been tempted to do that, wanting to feel his arm about her, tightening around her, hauling her against him; wanting him to dominate her, force her to do what he wanted; wanting to put his self-control to the test.

But she hadn't rushed towards the stairs. Instead she had turned and had walked back slowly to the dais, knowing that he hadn't been watching her. As she had stepped up on to the dais she had looked over her shoulder and had been unable to see him because he had been hidden by the drawing board. Slowly, very slowly, she had untied the belt of her robe and taking hold of it by the lapels had lifted it away from her body and let it slide from her shoulders down her arms to fall at her feet.

She had stood there almost petrified by her own temerity at daring to appear in the nude before a man she had known for such a short time, waiting for him to say something. Her arms had been stretched out and down, a little behind her body as the robe had slid from them, she had had one leg slightly in front of the other and her head had been tipped slightly back as she had stared unseeingly at the dimness beyond the glow of lamplight. She knew she had been standing like that, because later she had seen the quick sketch of her Rick had made while she had been frozen in that position.

He hadn't made any remark, and eventually she had moved of her own accord to do what he had suggested, miming the actions she went through every morning when she woke up, and in the process of remembering and reproducing the movements she had forgotten her shyness for a while. She had hardly been aware of Rick as he had sat at the easel beyond the circle of the lamplight. The only sound had been the rustle of paper when he had flicked it over to start a new sketch on a new sheet.

The timer pinging had startled her, and she had swung round then to peer at him.

'Okay, take a rest. Put your robe on.' He had spoken tersely. 'I'm going to get us something to drink. What would you like? Beer or lemonade?'

She had chosen lemonade, and after she had pulled on her robe had stepped down from the dais and had gone over to the easel to look at the sketches.

The first she had looked at had been disappointing to her unartistic eyes. It had seemed to be mostly scribble. She had turned the lifted sheets of paper back and had seen more puzzling scribbles until she had reached the first sheet of paper and had seen a more finished sketch of herself standing still just after she had dropped the robe.

Rick had come to her side and had offered a glass of lemonade in which ice had clinked.

'Recognise yourself?' he had asked.

'In this one, yes,' she had replied, glancing at him shyly. 'But the others just look like scribble.'

'Thanks,' he had retorted dryly, and had lifted the top sheet to reveal the sketch underneath. 'You were moving fairly quickly,' he explained, 'and this shows you sitting up—or rather it shows the movement of you sitting up.' He turned another page. 'This one shows the movements you make when you stretch.'

Turning to each sketch in turn, he explained what each one expressed.

'They're what I call gesture sketches. I'm trying to find out the meaning behind each movement you make rather than to put on paper what you look like. A gesture is something in its own right and I'll do as many as I can of your gestures until I'm aware of the way you move without having to actually see you move. I'm trying to get to know you thoroughly . . . so that when I come to use your figure in any sculpture I make, it will be there in my mind and at my fingertips. Do you understand?'

'I'm trying,' she had replied.

'For the rest of the morning I don't want you to move about so much. You'll hold each pose I suggest to you for about ten minutes. Tomorrow I'll do more detailed drawings, and you'll hold a pose for about twenty minutes at a time, returning to it after a rest.'

Somehow after that Lori had been able to relax much more, and when she had finished sitting for him they had lunched together. Then Rick had told her to run away and play, to do what she liked, because he had wanted to work on something else.

'Come back around five and we'll have something to eat and then you can pose again for an hour or two, when it's cooler.'

She hadn't really known what to do with

herself during the afternoon. She had wished there had been somewhere for her to swim and had thought of going down to the nearest beach, until she remembered that on that side of the island there would be surf. . . .

Cramp stabbed sharply through her leg again, and this time she couldn't help crying out. She rolled over and sat up quickly, rubbing the calf of her right leg, hearing Rick's crisp curses.

'I'm sorry, I couldn't stay in that position any longer,' she said, 'My leg is cramped.'

'All right, get up. Walk around,' he said curtly, not looking at her, his whole attention absorbed by what he had painted. 'We'll stop there and come back to it this evening. Like to get us some lunch?'

It was the first time he had suggested that she should make a meal, and she was surprisingly pleased to have something practical to do. In the small kitchen partitioned off from the rest of the studio she prepared tuna fish and salad sandwiches, tall glasses of iced tea and a bowl of fresh fruits, and putting everything on a tray carried it through to the studio. The blinds had been raised and the window and door had been opened. Bright sunlight poured into the big room.

'What would you like to do this afternoon?' Rick asked.

'I'd like to go swimming. Is there anywhere near here?'

'Only the pool at Denny's hotel. Or the one at Tamarind,' he replied. 'The best place to swim and snorkel is across the narrows in a bay on the southern tip of the island of Anadorada.'

'How would I get there?'

'The only way is by boat.' He gave her a slow, rather sultry glance. 'I guess I could take the afternoon off and we could charter a sailing sloop from the marina in Williamstown and sail over.'

'I know nothing about sailing,' she confessed.

'I do. Would you like to go?'

'Yes, yes, I would ... please. If it isn't too much trouble and ... and doesn't cost too much,' she replied politely.

'It won't be any trouble, and as to it costing anything ...' he paused, his lips curling in a slightly mysterious smile, 'it might turn out to be worth every dollar.'

The boat was about thirty feet long, had sleeping berths for four, a small galley and an auxiliary engine. They motored away from the marina docks and out into the bay towards the distant green hills which were the island of Anadorada. Rick showed her how to steer with the tiller and then left her in the cockpit while he hoisted the two sails. Returning to the cockpit, he pulled on ropes until the sails stopped flapping. The wind filled the two shining white triangles of cloth, the boat heeled over a little on one side and surged through the water. Rick stopped the engine and took the tiller from her.

'The wind is on the beam, so we won't have to change tacks,' he explained to her. 'We'll be there in about an hour and a half.'

Lori stretched out on one of the cockpit seats, her back resting against the cabin. Water chuckled beneath the hull of the boat, wind hummed in the rigging. Across the dancing brilliantly blue white-capped water Dorada rose green and purple, perfectly cone-shaped against the blue sky, the top of its mountain wreathed as usual with a gauzy scarf of pale grey cloud; a romantically mysterious island, a place where one could imagine dreams coming true.

This would be another time for her to remember, she thought when she returned to Canada. She glanced briefly at Rick. Sitting on the other cockpit seat, he was steering the boat, one large tanned hand on the tiller, and with his head tipped back he was watching one of the sails. Dark glasses shaded his eyes, the bleached strands of his hair glinted almost gold in the sunlight. Looking at him, she suddenly felt a warm tide of emotion flood through her. She wanted to go over and sit beside him, rest her head against his shoulder, put her arm about his waist and whisper to him *I want to stay with you for ever*.

She looked away sharply at the purple, cloud-hazed island and chewed on her lower lip. Ever since those moments on Denny's Beach when she had clung to him she had been fighting surges of desire like this, and during the last two days while she had been posing for him they had grown stronger and stronger. And now the two days' trial was almost over. Tomorrow she might have to leave.

She gave him another quick glance. Impossible for her to guess what he was thinking or feeling, as usual. Had he remembered that the two-day trial would end tonight? Had he found her to be a satisfactory model? He hadn't made any comment so far, but she knew that she hadn't been able to sit still for him as long as he had wanted her to this morning. He had shouted at her more than once and she had shouted back, much to her own surprise, and once had run from the dais and snatching her robe about her had run up the stairs to the bedroom and had stayed there until Rick had come and had insisted in a cool clipped voice that she go back down to the studio and sit again.

Instead of bringing them closer to each other, as she realised now she had hoped they would, the past day and a half seemed to have driven them farther apart. There was a tension between them now, even here on the boat; a tension which wouldn't ease until they had decided whether she wanted to stay longer and model for him and whether he wanted her to stay.

The bay at the southern tip of the small island of Anadorada was wide and open, sheltered from the wind and the swell of the sea by the other larger island. A beach of pale sand rimmed the curving shore and was backed by a thick green forest of trees which covered the two small hills. No other boat was anchored there and no houses or other signs of habitation crouched among the green foliage. The place was completely deserted save for two pelicans diving for fish in one corner where the water was deep green, reflecting the trees.

Rick anchored the boat close to the shore, went down into the cabin and returned wearing only swimming briefs and carrying snorkelling equipment for two. Lori removed the shirt and shorts she was wearing to appear in her swimsuit and listened as he explained to her how to use the snorkel. Soon they were both over the side, swimming in the unbelievably clear water, diving down beneath the surface, using the long black flippers they were wearing to propel themselves along, breathing in air through the snorkel tubes while they watched fish darting across the firm white sand beneath them.

After a while they swam to the shore and wandered in the forest where monkeys chattered and parrots squawked. Returning to the beach, they sat in the shade of a drooping palm tree. Immediately tension was back, twanging between them. They were too close physically for comfort, thought Lori, with a wry smile as she fought once again with the desire to reach out and touch Rick on his arm, brawny and tanned, covered with golden hairs which she could just see from beneath her lowered lids when she looked sideways; or on his thigh ... she looked away sharply, her breath catching in her throat audibly, and shifted away from him, trying to move stealthily, hoping he hadn't noticed. He did.

'What's wrong?' He spoke sharply.

'Nothing.' Lori tried to be casual as she lay down on the warm sand on her stomach and rested her head on her folded arms. That way she couldn't see him, but she was still tinglingly aware of him.

'Don't lie!' he growled, and she heard him move. He lay down beside her, on his back. His arm knocked against hers as he lifted it and put it behind his head, and she quivered uncontrollably. 'You're not comfortable posing, are you?' he asked. 'You still feel you're doing something you shouldn't do. You're all tensed up inside while you're doing it. That's why you're getting cramp so much.'

Silence followed, because Lori didn't know what to say. How could she tell him that she was tense because she was afraid, not of him, but of her own feelings when she was with him?

'Are the drawings you've done satisfactory?' she mumbled after a while.

'No, they're not. They're damned disappointing. I'd hoped. . . .' He broke off, then added with a touch of weariness, 'I guess I hoped for too much, expected too much. As usual.' Bitterness edged his voice.

Lori raised her head and glanced at him. Dappled with sunlight and shadow beneath the drooping frond of the palm tree, his face was set in hard lines. The corners of his mouth were drawn into a tight downward curve and his eyes were closed beneath his brows.

'I wish you'd tell me why you chose me to sit for you,' she whispered. 'Why me?'

He opened his eyes and slanted her a narrowed, glittering glance.

'Because you're like I imagined Emily Greville to have been,' he said.

'You mean the woman who threw herself out of the window after her husband had been killed in a duel?' she exclaimed.

'After her husband *and* her lover had been killed,' he said quietly. 'The story has fascinated me ever since I heard it. I want to tell it in sculpture.'

'Wouldn't it be easier to tell it in paintings or drawings?'

'Not for me. I see it as a series of scenes in sculpture. I'm a very physical person and so I have to express myself in sculpture. I like the primitive energy and brutality of wood or of huge blocks of stone. I love them and want to impose my will on them. They're not surfaces like canvas or paper on which I have to work with paint or charcoal. They're media with which I can create.' Lori must have expressed puzzlement on her face, because he broke off to laugh. 'Am I talking over your head, love?' he asked.

The casual endearment flicked her where it hurt. She lowered her head to her folded arms again, hiding her face.

'Don't call me that,' she muttered.

'What?'

'Don't call me love.'

'Why not?'

'Because . . . oh, because I'm not your love.'

'Yes, you are. I love you.' His voice held a light, taunting note.

'Oh, sure you do,' she retorted, raising her head again to glare at him. 'You love me like you love a piece of wood or granite, and you'd like to impose your will on me.'

'That's right, I do.' He was maddeningly equable in his agreement with her, and she felt she wanted to punch him. He lay down again, and closed his eyes. 'When I saw you at Sint Maarten looking all lost and forlorn as I had imagined Emily to have looked after the two men had been killed I had to sketch you. Then when I heard that your experience had been somewhat similar to hers, losing your husband soon after you'd married him, I wanted you to pose for me, to be Emily.'

But I'm not Emily, a voice cried within her. *I'm Lori, a real live woman, and I've got over the loss of my husband. I'm free of his shadow at last. I'm no longer damaged by what he did to me and I want to be loved, I want you to love me, not like you love a piece of wood or granite, not like you love the ghost of Emily Greville, but . . .*

'Where will you do the sculpting?' she asked hurriedly, shying away from her thoughts. In the two days she had been in his studio she hadn't seen any sculptures, only paintings and drawings and a few wood carvings.

'In Mexico. I have access to the stone I want to use there.'

'And when you're in Mexico will you . . . will you live with your wife?' She forced the words out in a husky whisper.

Rick was as still as stone for a few seconds, then he opened his eyes and looked at her.

'I don't have a wife,' he replied.

Lori pushed herself up into a sitting position, curling her legs under her, and stared down at him rebukingly.

'Now you're telling lies,' she accused.

He sat up too in one lithe movement. The action brought him very close to her. The green eyes glared into hers.

'No, I'm not,' he retorted. 'I don't have a wife.

Who told you I have?'

'Joan Bianco told me the other night that you married the daughter of your teacher Pablo Cosado some years ago.'

'Ha!' His laugh was short and mirthless. 'So I did. But how did Joan know that?'

'She said she'd read it in an American art magazine.'

'Ah, yes, I remember. There was an article published about me after my first exhibition in New York. But that was before I came to Dorada, over eight years ago.' He glanced away from her at the sea, his mouth twisting at one corner. 'My wife died just before I came here.'

'Oh! I'm sorry.' A strange relief was flooding through her easing tension. 'Was she in an accident?'

His glance came back to her. The twist of his lips became more marked, more sardonic.

'I guess I'll have to tell you the whole dreary story, won't I?' he said, the expression in his eyes softening as he studied her face. 'You're not going to be happy until I do. You've been worrying about it ever since Joan told you, haven't you? That's why you've been so tense.' His face hardened again. 'Hell, why did she have to drop a piece of information like that?' he grated. 'She talks too much. Yak, yak, yak!'

'I liked her,' said Lori, tilting her chin at him, and he smiled at her. He raised a hand as if to touch her face in a caress, then changed his mind and let his hand drop and looked away from her at the sea again, frowning a little. 'What was your wife's name?' she asked, her voice shaking a little with disappointment because he hadn't touched her.

'Stella,' he said curtly. 'She was an artist too. I met her when I went to study with Cosada about eleven years ago. We were attracted to each other.' He paused, his frown deepening, and let out a weary sigh. 'But she wanted to be married, so we were married,' he added in a colourless tone, taking a handful of the fine almost white sand and letting the grains trickle through his fingers.

'Didn't you want to be married?'

He looked at her over his shoulder, his expression cynical.

'No, I didn't. But Stella was very beautiful and very persuasive, so we were married.' He shrugged his broad shoulders and looked away from her. 'A year later she asked for a separation with a view to getting a divorce,' he continued in cold clipped tones. 'I agreed, because it was obvious to me I'd made a mistake in getting married. I left Mexico and went to Italy to study for a year with Manzini. When I went back to Mexico to see Stella about getting a divorce I was told she was in hospital dying of cancer.'

'Oh, how awful!' gasped Lori. 'What did you do?'

'I stayed near the hospital and visited her every day until she died,' he said heavily. 'Afterwards her sister told me Stella had asked for a separation only because she'd found out she was incurably ill.' He paused. The short silence was loaded with suppressed emotion. When he continued his voice was very low, almost inaudible. 'She hadn't wanted me to know because she'd guessed I would stay with her even though I was finding our marriage restrictive. She had realised our uneasy relationship was coming between me and my art, so she'd decided to free me from it.'

There was another silence. The water lapped softly at the sand; birds squawked in the forest behind them.

'She must have been a very good person, truly unselfish,' said Lori at last.

'She was, too good for a self-interested ambitious bastard like me,' he growled.

'And she must have loved you very much to let you go,' she added.

He gave her another sardonic glance over his shoulder, then rose to his feet.

'I guess she did,' he drawled dryly. 'I'm going diving again to see if I can get some fish for our supper. Coming?'

Lori shook her head and watched him stride away to the edge of the beach. She needed to be alone for a few minutes to think about what he had told her. Rick put on the flippers and waded out into the water, then fitted the mask and snorkel tube over his face and slid under the surface.

The shadows of the trees were growing longer and blacker and Dorada had almost disappeared in the blue haze of early evening. In the bay the water was calm, smooth and golden where the sun still shone on it, a dark greenish blue in the shadow of the land. The boat was still, its reflection in the water so perfect that there were two boats, one right way up the other upside down.

Leaving the shade of the palm, Lori lay down again on warm sand and closed her eyes. Rick hadn't liked telling her about his marriage to Stella Cosada, and she could understand why. The picture the story had presented of him was not impressive. Perhaps he had been warning her about himself; warning her not to try and trap him in a possessive relationship. But even so she was glad he had told her, because now she knew he no longer had a wife hidden away in Mexico, she could feel more at ease with him when he asked her to stay longer and pose for him. She frowned. That was if he wanted her to stay. He might have decided she was no good as a model.

The sun's rays warmed her right cheek, right arm and right leg. Water sighed softly, the only sound. Her eyes closed and her thoughts became vague and hazy, then faded altogether in the grey mist of sleep.

She wakened abruptly, blinking her eyes, aware that her skin had cooled and that water was lapping at her feet. She sat up quickly. The sun was going down and the water was streaked with pink and gold. The tide was making slowly and silently and would soon be up to the rocks behind her. She stood up and dusted sand from her limbs. She was alone on the beach.

There was no sign of Rick anywhere and she wondered if he had returned to the boat after fishing. Fitting on her flippers, she waded out into the water, put on mask and snorkel and swam out to the boat. She managed to clamber aboard and took off the snorkelling gear. No one came out of the cabin to greet her.

Rick wasn't on the boat. Standing on the foredeck, Lori surveyed the flat water of the bay, searching for the telltale ripples made by a snorkel tube or the movement of a swimmer's flippers. But the play the light and shadow made it difficult to see any movement.

Where was Rick? She should have asked him which part of the bay he had intended to fish in. Or he should have told her. Quickly she returned to the cockpit and put on the flippers again, then the mask and the snorkel, and jumped into the water. She swam all round the bay, peering under the surface of the water until it became too dark to see anything on the bottom, then she surfaced and waded ashore to rest against a rock and to catch her breath.

The sun had set and the water was silvery. The sky was a pale greenish grey scattered with dark blue clouds edged with an apricot colour, the last of the sunset glow. In the distance Dorada was now hazy purple and lights twinkled at the base of the mountain, the lights of Williamstown.

Some animal squawked harshly in the forest, startling her. Lori pushed away from the rock and looked fearfully around her, feeling the beginning of panic niggling in her stomach.

Where was Rick? Was he still fishing? No, he couldn't be, because he wouldn't be able to see under water. Was he on the shore somewhere? Why hadn't he come back to her? Why didn't he call to her?

Stepping to the edge of the water, she cupped

her hands about her mouth and shouted his name several times, then paused to listen. No voice called back to her. She shouted again. No reply, only the moan of the wind in the trees, the squawks and twitters of monkeys and birds, the mocking gurgle of water among rocks.

The boat was rapidly becoming one with the darkness that was creeping across the sky and the sea. If she didn't swim back to it soon she might not be able to find it. But where was Rick? Surely he hadn't drowned? Surely he hadn't sucked in water instead of air when he dived deeply. Oh, God no! Panic was a sickness now, weakening her, making her want to cry out, to take her head in her hands and moan in an agony of loss. He couldn't have drowned. He mustn't have drowned. She couldn't bear to lose him now that she had just discovered she loved him and wanted him; now that she had discovered there was nothing to stop her from loving him and wanting him.

She gulped down the panic, put the flippers on again, but didn't fit the mask and snorkel tube properly, just wore them on her head so that her hands would be free to swim. When she waded into the water it sparkled with phosphorescence. She dived and swam strongly towards the boat.

The cockpit was empty. No light shone out from the cabin. All was quiet except for the slap of a halliard against the metal mast. Rick wasn't there. Lori pulled off the flippers and mask and threw them down, looking around wildly at the dark uncaring water, the darker unfeeling land, the mocking stars winking in the sky.

'Rick, oh, Rick, where are you? Where are you?' she sobbed, collapsing on one of the cockpit seats, giving way to panic at last. 'Oh, please don't be drowned!' she cried nonsensically. 'I couldn't bear it if you were drowned. Please come back to the boat. Please, please come back now!'

What if he didn't come back? What if she never found him? How would she get back to Williamstown to ask for help in searching for him? Wiping her tears away with her fingers, she sat up, panic retreating before practical thought as she tried to remember what he had done to start the engine. There was something to be done with switches on a panel in the cabin. If she remembered rightly the panel was to the left of the steps.

She groped her way through the hatchway and down the steps. Her fingers found the panel. She flicked switches, hoping that one of them would bring light to the cabin. Behind her Rick said dryly,

'Try the top switch on the right.'

She gasped and whirled, to come up against his muscular naked body, her bare arms brushing against his bare chest. He was a warm pulsing presence, his skin scented with salt water and other more mysterious male scents.

'Why didn't you let on you were here?' she demanded shrilly, glaring up at him through the dimness.

'I thought you'd get around to coming down here after a while and would find me,' he said softly.

Fury fused with relief. He had been here all the

time while she had been panic-stricken in the cockpit, crying for him to come back to her.

'You devil, you were here all the time and I thought you'd drowned! Oh, oh . . .!' She could contain her emotions no longer. Raising her fists, she beat at his bare chest. He caught and held her wrists, putting her arms behind her back, at the same time drawing her towards him. Her head tipped backwards, her body arched involuntarily in invitation, her breasts swelled and hardened.

'Did you mean what you said,' he whispered, 'about not being able to bear it if I'd drowned?'

'Oh yes, I meant it. I meant it,' she moaned in an agony of desire.

'So you care about what happens to me?'

'I care. I care very much.' she sighed.

He let go of her wrists then and his arms went round her. His lips found hers in the darkness and they kissed hungrily and often, with warmth and abandon, exulting in being close to each other. Her hands stroked his back, loving the feel of his skin still damp from swimming. His lips slid from her mouth to her cheek up to her temple, to her eyes and back to her mouth. His hands smoothed and squeezed her, then slowly peeled the wet swimsuit from her skin and she was pressed against him, moulded against his naked body.

'I can't be this close to you without wanting you,' he whispered.

'And I can't be close to you like this without wanting you,' she replied shyly, her lips moving against his throat.

'So it's a mutual feeling.'

'It's mutual.'

'Then what are we waiting for?' he said on a note of triumph, and, lifting her, carried her into the main part of the cabin and put her down on the berth which could be pulled out to make a sleeping place for two.

'You're not afraid any more?' he said, gathering her against him. 'You're not afraid of what we're going to do?'

'Now I want to do it. Show me how,' she whispered.

Slowly, tenderly his hands caressed every part of her, and where his hands had been his lips followed, drawing from her a response which swelled up and burst through the bonds of her shyness, overwhelming and obliterating all thoughts. Swamped by her own passion, Lori didn't care any more if it was light or dark, whether it was warm or cold, as long as she could hold him, closer and closer and closer, until they fused together in an explosion of joy.

Later she was roused from the delicious lethargy induced by satisfaction by the touch of his fingers against her jaw. She opened her eyes to the soft glow of an oil lamp swinging in brass gimbals. She was lying nude under a thin blanket which Rick had thrown over her and he was sitting on the side of the berth, dressed in shirt and shorts, his hair haloed round his head by the lamplight, his face in the shadows, enigmatic.

'Would you like some supper?' he asked, and she became aware of the smell of fish being cooked.

'You did catch some, then?'

'Of course I did. Are you hungry?'

'Starving!' She avoided his penetrating stare. After what had happened so recently between them, after the wild abandon of the past hour, she felt even more shy of him. He had roused in her a sensuality which secretly amazed her. Yet he seemed no different. 'What time is it?' she asked.

'About nine o'clock.'

'Are we going to stay here all night?'

'We'll go back to the marina as soon as we've eaten.'

'In the dark?' she exclaimed. 'How will we see?'

'I've got cat's eyes, or hadn't you noticed?' he mocked, ruffling her hair with a hand, as if she were an inquisitive child. 'We'll be able to see. There are stars to light the way and I promised to return the boat before midnight. If I don't I'll have to pay for another half day's charter.' He rose to his feet. 'Your shorts and shirt are on the bunk in the forward cabin,' he added, and went back to the stove in the galley to look at the frying fish.

Lori slid from the berth and went through to the other cabin. When she returned to the main cabin the double berth had been folded back into its daytime arrangement as a single berth settee, the blanket had disappeared and the table was set.

They sat side by side to eat. The fish were white-fleshed, firm and deliciously flavoured.

'Where did you find them?' asked Lori.

'In a deep pool, over by the northern headland.'

'You weren't on the boat the first time I came out to it,' she said, 'so I swam round the bay looking for you.'

'I know,' he replied.

'You saw me? Then why didn't you call to me?'

'I'd just noticed the fish, so I had to dive for them. When I got to the boat you'd left it, so I swam to the shore where we'd been sitting and you weren't there. I guessed you'd turn up sooner or later, so I came back to the boat to have a sleep. I woke up to hear you muttering and sobbing to yourself.' The kettle on the stove began to whistle. He stood. 'Like some coffee?'

'Yes, please,' she muttered. She still felt cross with him for being so unconcerned about her he had been able to sleep while she had been searching for him in panic. He came back to the table with two mugs of coffee, set them down and sat beside her again.

'The two-day trial is almost over,' he said in his abrupt way. 'Do you want to catch the early morning plane to Sint Maarten?'

'Do . . . do you want me to catch it?' she asked shakily. Nothing had changed after all. The joyous culmination of passion which they had experienced together had made no difference to his feelings. 'You said you weren't satisfied with the drawings you had made of me, and I think perhaps it's my fault they're no good, because I'm not a very good model,' she added in a low voice.

'It is your fault they're no good,' Rick said bluntly, and she turned to glare at him, annoyed with him for agreeing with her. He grinned at her shamelessly. 'You were terrible this morning, tense to the point of stiffness, and I was getting all sorts of nasty vibrations from you. I could *feel* your suspicions of me.' He leaned forward and placed a hand on her thigh, then slowly he began to stroke it. 'But now I know why you were like that,' he said softly, 'so I'm hoping that now you know I don't have a wife in Mexico you'll be more relaxed.' His fingers slid tantalisingly over her knee as he leaned closer. His eyes glinted with tender mockery. 'And then making love the way we did does have a certain therapeutic value. You're not hating me any more,' he added wickedly.

'Is that why you made love to me?' she demanded furiously.

'Perhaps,' he teased, then laughed as he caught hold of the hand she had raised to slap him. 'No, that isn't why. We made love because we couldn't help it, because we've fallen in love with each other, and if you stay to pose for me longer we'll make love again. Are you going to take that risk? Are you going to stay?'

'How long?' she whispered, swaying towards him mesmerised by the green flames of desire flickering in his eyes, feeling the red-hot passion flood through her again.

'Two weeks?' he suggested on a note of enquiry, his lips barely an inch from hers as his hand slid up from her thigh up over the curve of her hip and waist to cup her breast.

'I'll stay,' she agreed breathlessly, and surrendered once again to the touch of desire.

CHAPTER SEVEN

IN the small departure lounge at the airport in
Sint Maarten the air was hot and humid. Sweat
was beginning to shine on the faces of the many
tourists who were crammed into the room.
Outside, sunlight glittered on the runways and on
the wings of planes. Little white clouds rolled
lazily across the brilliant blue sky.

Lori sat in a corner waiting to be called to
board the plane for Miami. She looked at the
people who were sitting near to her. There was a
young woman holding hands with a young man.
They were seemingly engrossed with each other.
Occasionally the young woman would spread out
the fingers of her left hand and gaze admiringly at
the gold band on her third finger which gleamed
below the blaze of a diamond set in another gold
band. Honeymooners.

Lori's gaze drifted past them to the black man
who sat beside the couple. His chestnut-coloured
eyes were dreamy and he was humming a tune to
himself while his right foot tapped on the floor in
rhythm. His shirt was a gaudy Palm Beach print
and his pants were pink. Gold chains glittered
against his smooth brown neck. He wasn't at all
like Sylvester, but her glance slid past him
hopefully and stopped. No husky suntanned man
with sun-bleached unruly hair, wearing faded
blue denims, sat there. Only a plump black

woman in a bright cotton dress, a printed scarf tied round her head, nursing a baby and crooning to it softly.

But why should she hope to see Rick, when she knew he had gone? When barely half an hour ago he had left her with a kiss on her cheek and a careless wave of his hand as he had stepped out of the lounge on his way to board a plane bound for Texas? He had gone to Mexico, and she didn't even know the name of the place where he had his other studio, because she had forgotten to ask for his address and he hadn't bothered to tell her. He had gone, and it was over, their brief tropical affair, and now she felt worse than she had felt after Mark had died. She felt she wanted to die. Like Emily Greville, she had no husband and no lover, and being alive seemed suddenly futile.

The flight to Miami was called and she joined the tourists listlessly to board the plane. The flight was smooth, uneventful. At Miami, after a short wait, she boarded another plane for Montreal, moving automatically in the right direction, taking her place in the right seat, then sitting without speaking, almost without seeing, a slim, quiet young woman who seemed calm and composed until you looked into her eyes and saw the anguish in their dark brown depths.

It was late, almost eleven-thirty, when at last she left the plane on which she had flown from Montreal to her home town, and hurried through icy blasts of wind laden with a few flakes of snow towards the small terminal building.

'Lori! It's great to see you!' Kathy was there,

dressed for bad weather in slacks, quilted hooded parka and boots. 'They said the plane might not be able to land ... the weather being bad. They said you might have to go on to Halifax and be bussed back here. Have we had weather since you went away! Loads of snow. You don't know what you've missed. Oh, look, there's Sheila Pratt. She's back from a trip to the Bahamas. Hey, Sheila? How are you doing? Like a drive into town with us?'

Lori sat in the back seat of Kathy's small two-door Japanese car, glad to let Sheila Pratt sit beside Kathy on the drive into the town. The surface of the road was slippery and huge banks of snow lined the sides of it, piled up there by snow-ploughs. In the distance, ahead, spread out on the humpy hills around its harbour, the city glittered with lights. She was back home, only never again would it seem like home to her, because the person she wanted to be with most didn't live there, would never live there.

The apartment was just the same, but why should it be different? She'd been away only a month, after all.

'I wasn't surprised to hear you were on your way back when you called today from Miami,' said Kathy as she booted the door closed behind her and began to unzip her parka. 'I read about Mrs Bernice Alden's death in the paper.'

'She died?' gasped Lori in surprise, swinging round to face her friend.

'You didn't know?' exclaimed Kathy, her eyebrows going up. 'But surely ...?' She broke off and frowned.

'I . . . I knew she was ill, but I didn't think she would die,' said Lori quickly. 'She . . . she was taken away to hospital in Florida two weeks ago and I hadn't heard anything more about her.'

'How come?' Still obviously puzzled, Kathy slid off her parka and tossed it over the back of a chair, then sitting down in the same chair, she began to pull off her boots.

'I hadn't seen anyone from Tamarind for two weeks,' mumbled Lori, taking off her suit jacket. 'After she was taken away, I was sacked . . . by Clarke Alden.'

'You were?' Kathy's eyes opened wide. 'Then what have you been doing for two weeks?'

Lori sank down on the old chesterfield and pushed her hair back wearily. The numbness which had shut her off from pain ever since Rick had left her that morning was beginning to wear off. She was starting to hurt and she wanted to hide away, crawl into her bed, pull the covers over her head and to cry her heart out.

'I've been working for an artist . . . a sculptor,' she said, and her voice was surprisingly cool and even. 'I posed for him while he did some drawings of me.'

'In the nude?' squeaked Kathy, her eyes growing even wider. '*You?*'

'Yes, me.' Lori couldn't help laughing a little at her friend's astonishment.

'My God!' exclaimed Kathy. 'Wonders will never cease!' She leaned forward eagerly, avid for more information. 'What was he like? Was he young?'

'Mid-thirties.'

'Handsome?'

'In a way. He was big, suntanned.'

'A playboy?' Kathy's eyes twinkled.

'Not really.'

'And did you . . . did he. . . .?'

'We had an affair, yes,' said Lori. And rose to her feet. 'I'm ready for bed,' she said, drifting over towards her bedroom. 'What's the job situation like, Kathy? I suppose I'll have to start looking tomorrow.'

'Same as it was when you went away. You haven't been away all that long, you know.'

'Seems like months,' sighed Lori.

'They haven't replaced you at the museum yet. You might try there first.' Kathy tipped her head to one side, her glance inquisitive. 'Why did he want you to pose for him? Did he draw pictures of you?'

'He made sketches and some finished drawings, also two paintings, and he's going to make sculptures using them as guides. He's gone to Mexico to do that.'

'*Wow!*' exclaimed Kathy. 'Will the sculptures or the paintings ever be exhibited?'

'I'm not sure. He didn't say.' Lori stifled another yawn. 'Thanks for coming to meet me, Kathy. See you tomorrow. Goodnight.'

In bed she lay and looked at the pale glow of street lamplight through the window which she had left uncurtained and thought about Rick. Last night they had slept together in the quaint circular bedroom above his studio at the sugar mill. Every night since the afternoon they had spent at the bay on Anadorada Island they had slept together, sometimes making love, sometimes just sleeping. Every morning she had posed for him, completely at ease at last, contented to be there with him. And every afternoon she had spent alone while he had been busy with other artistic pursuits or had ridden off in the jeep somewhere, never asking her to go with him.

She had known that the time with him would come to an end inevitably, when he had done enough drawings of her, yet she had hoped right up to the moment of parting at Sint Maarten airport that morning that he might ask her to go with him to Mexico; a foolishly romantic hope, because there was no reason why he should have asked her to go with him. They'd made no promises to each other, no commitment beyond two weeks.

Their love for each other had been free—freely given and freely taken. She had stayed and posed for him because she had loved him, and he had asked her to stay and live with him for the two weeks because he had loved her. But now it was over. She turned on to her side and closed her eyes on the tears which had welled in them. There would be no regrets, she vowed determinedly. To waste time in regret would be to spoil the memories she had of living with Rick.

Next day she went to the museum and was given her old job back, her boss in the history department seeming to be actually relieved to see her. By the end of the week she was settled in the old groove, but though the groove was the same she wasn't. Her adventure in Dorada had drawn her out of the shell in which she had been hiding since Mark had died, forcing her out of it, and never would she return to it.

No longer repressed, sure of herself as a woman who had come to terms with her femininity, she no longer sat at home every evening. As spring passed and gave way to summer she went out and about with friends, joined in, learned to play tennis, took a course in sailing on the river, met people, made new friends, and by the time the leaves were turning crimson, yellow and bronze she was being dated regularly by Terry Johnson whom she had known at the firm of accountants where she had worked for Mark.

Terry wasn't unlike Mark, as Kathy was quick to point out in warning. Dark-haired, with neat clear-cut features, he was punctual and attentive, polite but reserved, perhaps a little cold. At Christmas he proposed marriage to Lori.

His proposal startled her, stopped her short and made her realise what path she was treading again. Her answer came quickly without conscious thought and she knew it had been there in her mind ever since she had met him.

'No. No, thank you,' she said. 'I don't want to be married again—not just yet. Please don't ask me again.'

He was annoyed and showed it, and had the nerve to tell her she didn't know her own mind— and he did ask her again, annoying her considerably.

'I've given you my answer and I'm not going to change my mind,' she retorted. 'I don't want to marry you.'

'Why not? I've got a good job, I could buy a house immediately, there'd be no living in a tiny apartment for us to start with. You could give up your job—I'd want you to stay at home anyway.'

'And be there when you come home from work with your meal all ready and your shirt washed for the next day,' she had added mockingly. 'No thank you. I couldn't live with you, Terry—I'm sorry, but I couldn't.'

'Want to be a widow all your life?' he jeered, obviously offended. 'Want to live alone without a man?'

'Yes,' she replied quietly. 'If I can't live with the man I love, I do want to live alone. Goodbye.'

It had been the end of their association, and afterwards she was careful not to be dated by any of the men she met. Christmas passed and the New Year came in, bringing with it the real winter weather. She bought cross-country skis and discovered the winter countryside with Kathy. She joined a curling club and played on an all-woman team. She went to an evening class at the university campus and learned basic drawing, trying to sketch on rough paper with French *conté* chalk the young woman who posed in the nude for the class.

And every day, every night she thought about Rick, wishing she had an address she could write to, wishing he would write to her, wondering if she would ever hear from him, wondering if they would ever meet again.

Only if she went back to Dorada. The idea was insidious, burrowing into her mind and taking root there as January gave way to February and everyone began to talk about taking a week off to go south; to Florida or the Bahamas; to Bermuda or Antigua or Barbados, anywhere where the weather was warmer and they could relax for a few days, re-charge their batteries so that they could survive the rest of the winter.

She could go to Dorada for a week's holiday, on a package tour, she discovered when she enquired from Kathy's friend Cindy, who worked at the local travel agency. She could stay for six days and nights in one of those exclusive hotels Rick had talked about, and she had just persuaded Kathy to agree to go with her when the invitation came.

It was the only mail to arrive one day and it lay on the table in the living room of the apartment where Kathy had put it when she had arrived home a few minutes before Lori.

'For you,' said Kathy, pointing to it. 'From Washington, D.C.'

'Must be an advertisement for something,' Lori said, suppressing her disappointment because it wasn't from Mexico or Dorada. She picked up the square cream envelope. Her name and address had been typewritten and the Stevens had been spelt incorrectly with a 'ph' instead of a 'v'. In the left-hand corner of the envelope the return address was a post office box number in Washington.

She slit it open. There was a stiff card inside. She drew it out and stared at it. Her heart beat fast, her cheeks grew hot, the blood boiled in her veins.

'What is it?' demanded Kathy, noting the

change in her face. She bounced across the room to stand behind Lori and to look down at the card. She read the words on the card, muttering them aloud. 'You are cordially invited to attend the opening of an exhibition of recent drawings, sculptures and paintings, 'Images of Dorada', by Patrick Greville at the Broughton Gallery, Washington D.C., on March First. There will be a reception at which the artist will be present. This card admits two.' Kathy drew breath, then burst out excitedly, 'It's from him, isn't it. The artist you posed for? Lori, turn the card over. There's something written on the back.'

Lori turned the card with shaking hands and stared at the sloping handwriting.

'Lori,' she read, 'I hope you'll be there on March the First. Come and see Emily. All my love, Rick.'

'You're going, of course,' breathed Kathy enthusiastically.

'I ... I'm not sure.'

'I am. I'm going with you. It says the card admits two.'

'But. . . .'

'Come on, we'll go and see Cindy now,' said Kathy, pulling on her parka. 'We'll go to Washington instead of Dorada.'

'But I'm not sure,' bleated Lori weakly, still staring at Rick's handwriting. He hadn't forgotten her, and he had sent his love. He wanted her to be at his exhibition, yet she was strangely reluctant to go and see the sculptures he had done of her as Emily Greville. 'Someone might recognise me,' she muttered vaguely, 'and that would be embarrassing.'

'So what?' retorted Kathy. 'Who cares? Oh, come on, Lori! The travel agency is open on Friday night. Cindy can tell us the best way to get to Washington and if there are any cheap deals for a weekend at a hotel.'

The day of the opening of the exhibition was a Sunday, so they flew to Washington by way of Boston on the Saturday before to stay at a hotel near the airport. After settling into their double room they decided to forgo dinner at the hotel and to go sightseeing instead, because someone had told Kathy that Washington was worth seeing at night.

Two elegant floodlit structures glowed among the tracery of dark bare branches and were reflected in the smooth waters of the Potomac River; both classical in design with sleek Greek pillars; the Jefferson monument all harmony and grace and round with a small dome; the Lincoln rectangular and severe, its rows of columns illuminated from behind. Beyond them a finger of stone, also floodlit, pointed to the starlit sky, seeming to pierce it—the Washington memorial, stern and commanding.

Stars twinkled too in the reflecting pools which were strung out along a wide road called the Mall and on top of its hill the Capitol building, more columns and a dome, seemed to float above the darkened city like an enchanted palace. Down from the hill into the town again, past the White House, more floodlit pillars, more grace and harmony, and along the streets of Georgetown, past neat houses built of mellow brick set behind brick sidewalks, past quaint boutiques and enormous mansions. It was a district where, so their taxi-driver guide told them, the rich and famous lived as well as the glamorous and the notorious.

Returning to the hotel, they ate sandwiches in the coffee bar and then went to bed. Lori couldn't sleep. She kept thinking of Rick, wondering where he was staying the night. The hours passed slowly, wheeling by her in a series of confused images—memories of the circular rooms of the sugar mill in Dorada, of the palm-shaded beaches and glittering blue sea, of brilliant blossoms in the garden at Tamarind, of the cone-shaped mountain, all mingling with the recent impressions of the cool classical structures of the American capital city.

Next morning they got up late and ate brunch at the hotel, then took a taxi to the gallery. It was in an old restored building on a corner of Pennsylvania Avenue and one of the many numbered streets which cross that main artery at right angles, and the chatty taxi driver told them that an artist had to be good to be exhibited there.

Many cars were parked on the street, and as they went up the steps Lori felt her innate shyness almost overcome her. She entered the high wide entrance hall timidly, hiding behind Kathy.

'I wonder where we'll find the sculptures of you,' said Kathy, looking at the catalogue which had been handed to them.

'Shush!' whispered Lori, looking round at the people who were standing about the hall holding glasses of wine. They were all talking loudly.

'No one will hear me in this crush,' said Kathy. She scowled at the catalogue. 'It says there are three sculptures of a woman's figure in Gallery Two.' She looked up at the doorway opening of the hallway. 'That's over there. Come on.'

The high-ceilinged room was long and wide. Its walls were painted pale grey and the woodwork was white. It was lit by long windows at either end. It was full of people, men in suits, women in winter dresses or suits, although there were some arty types Lori noticed with long hair and long skirts, or long hair, long beard and tatty jeans. At the end of the room there was a group standing silently staring at three almost life-sized female figures sculpted from some fine stone, the colour of pale gold. Lori and Kathy joined the awe-struck group and stared too at the beautifully carved forms, the rounded limbs, the slender curves of hips and shoulders, the uptilted breasts. To Lori's relief there was no detail on the faces of the sculptures. They were entirely representational and could have been any woman, yet still they were exquisitely carved. It was to the bodies that the eye was drawn time after time because of the emotion they expressed.

Lori fumbled with her catalogue and found the right page and read the description. All it said was that the exhibit was entitled: EMILY.

Lori looked again at the figures. One seemed to express hopeful serenity. One was ecstatic, the body arched back, arms flung wide in abandon.

One was dejected, sitting with shoulders slumped. She recognised herself in each of them.

'He must have known the model intimately to have been able to capture the expression of such intense emotions. No woman reveals her secret soul in public,' said a woman behind Lori.

'I wonder who she is,' said a male voice.

'Best work he's done—really great!' said another male voice. 'Reminiscent of Cosada, in its simplicity.'

'I can detect the influence of Manzini in the eroticism of the second figure. Didn't he study with both of them?'

'I can't agree with either of you. These are pure Greville,' said the woman. 'He's arrived as a sculptor, and I'm going to say so in my column in tomorrow's paper. He'd been inspired when he created these figures.'

'Inspired by what?' said one of the men with a sly chuckle. 'By the model? I wouldn't mind meeting her—I'd be inspired by a body like that!'

'He won't say who she is. I've asked him,' said another voice.

'Keeping her for himself, no doubt,' said the sly voice, chuckling again. 'Don't blame him either. She's quite a dish!'

Lori turned blindly, her cheeks burning, then pushed past the people behind her and hurried across the room to the hallway, hearing Kathy calling after.

'Hey, Lori—Lori, where are you going?'

'Yes, where are you going, Lori?' asked a beloved, slightly mocking voice as she collided with someone.

She looked up, saw greenish eyes in a suntanned, hard-bitten face laughing down at her, saw sun-bleached hair not as unruly as usual. Someone had made him wear a tie with the dark blue shirt he was wearing and the knot had been pulled loose as if he had found it too confining. He was wearing a grey tweed sports jacket too, and dark grey pants. He looked almost, but not quite, respectable.

'You came after all. I was so afraid you wouldn't come,' he murmured. 'Where are you staying, and for how long?'

'We're staying at a hotel near the airport.' She couldn't stop staring at him, but it seemed he couldn't stop staring at her either.

'We?' He frowned at her and snapped jealously, 'Who else?'

'Kathy and I.' She turned away from him to Kathy, who was standing just behind her. 'Kathy, I'd like you to meet Rick Greville. Kathy and I share an apartment,' she added, turning back to Rick. 'And we go home tomorrow.'

'I'll get your things picked up and brought to the hotel where I'm staying,' said Rick after he had greeted Kathy. 'You'll stay tonight with me.'

'No,' said Lori firmly. 'I can't.'

He had taken hold of her hand and he squeezed it hard as he smiled down at her and said softly.

'Yes, you can.'

'But what about Kathy? I can't just leave her on her own at the other hotel! If it wasn't for her I wouldn't have come. If it wasn't for her I would never have gone to Dorada,' babbled Lori, aware now that they were being stared at by people who had probably recognised Rick as being the creator of the works in the exhibition.

'So Kathy can move too.' He grinned at the suddenly and surprisingly silent Kathy, who seemed to have been struck dumb. 'Seems I owe you a lot, Kathy,' he told her. 'You won't mind moving into a room of your own at the Mayflower Hotel for tonight, will you?' Kathy could only shake her head negatively, signifying that she didn't mind, and Rick said, 'Good. Now let's go and find Henry.'

They found Henry, a small dapper man in a neat navy blue pinstripe suit, in another room where Rick's huge colourful paintings of Doradian scenes blazed on the pale walls.

'Henry, this is Lori, the model for those figures. I want her and her friend Kathy here moved to the Mayflower for tonight,' said Rick, at his most autocratic. 'Can it be done?'

'Surely,' said Henry. 'It is a pleasure to meet you at last ... Emily,' he purred, his eyes twinkling knowledgeably. 'What do you think of the figures? Have you seen them yet?'

'I. . . .' Lori started to speak, when she was interrupted by a burly young man who was wearing spectacles and who pushed past Henry to plant himself before her. He had a notebook in his hand.

'Did I hear Henry call you Emily?' he demanded. His eyes, covered by the thick-lensed glasses, surveyed her closely.

'I think it's time you and I got out of here,' muttered Rick, his hand tightening on hers. 'No, her name is Lori,' he said to the reporter. 'Not

Emily. She isn't Emily. Henry, take Kathy to their hotel and pay the bill and bring their things to the Mayflower. We'll see you both there later.'

He swung round then and pulling Lori after him made for the hallway. Several people tried to stop him, presumably to speak to him about the exhibits, but he ignored them and strode on. At last they were through the front door of the building and going down the steps. The sharp March wind whipped at their faces.

'Who's Henry?' Lori gasped as she almost ran to keep up with his strides.

'Henry Broughton. He's my dealer in the States and he owns the gallery, as well as others in New York and Minneapolis. He arranged the exhibition.'

'The taxi driver on the way here told us you have to be good, really good, to be exhibited at the Broughton,' she said as they stopped at a crossing and waited for the lights to change. Pale sunlight filtered through the bare branches of trees and glinted on the stone buildings.

'I am good,' Rick retorted with that brash self-confidence which always made her laugh. He slanted a glance down at her. 'Don't you like the sculptures I've done of you?'

'Don't you mean the sculptures you've done of Emily?' she taunted gently, and he grinned at her. 'I think they're beautiful,' she said inadequately. 'But they're not what I expected.'

He gave her a sharp glance but made no comment. The lights changed and they crossed the road. They walked across the small Lafayette Park. The White House gleamed softly in the pale sunlight. Along another street and down another. Rick still held her hand, but they didn't talk, and Lori wondered if she had upset him by what she had said about the sculptures.

It was a relief to enter the warmth of the hotel foyer after walking in the cold wind. In the elevator they stood silently with other people. On the third floor they got out and walked along a carpeted corridor. Rick unlocked a door and they entered a pleasant room furnished with discreet slightly old-fashioned elegance. There was a king-sized bed and on a table by the window there was an arrangement of spring flowers, and a tray with a basket of fresh fruit and a bottle of wine on it.

Still holding her hand, Rick swung her round to face him. His arms went around her and he hugged her tightly.

'I've missed you, love,' he whispered, rubbing his cheek against hers. Then his lips covered hers in a kiss whose rough passionate hunger left her in no doubts as to his feelings about her being with him.

'I've missed you too,' she said when the kiss was over and she was leaning back against the circle of his arms.

'Why haven't you written to me, then?' he demanded.

'I didn't have an address to write to! I didn't know where you were in Mexico—you didn't tell me where you were going.'

'I didn't?' He frowned perplexedly and letting go of her raked his hair with his fingers. He loosened his tie and took it off, to throw it carelessly on the floor, then he slipped off the tweed jacket and tossed it towards a chair. It missed the chair, of course, and Lori went forward to pick it up and lay it on the chair. 'I must have forgotten,' he muttered as he walked over to the window by the table. He picked up the wine bottle, took out the cork and poured wine into two glasses. 'Or I must have assumed you knew where I was going,' he added, coming across to her. 'Take off your coat. You are staying, you know.'

Lori slipped off her fur-collared coat and laid it on top of his jacket.

'Why didn't you write to me?' she asked as she took the glass of wine he offered to her.

'Same reason. I didn't have your address,' he replied with a gleam of humour. 'You forgot to give it to me. You could have written to me at Dorada, you know. It would have been sent on. Why didn't you?'

'I . . . wasn't sure,' she muttered evasively, then added more strongly, looking straight at him, 'I didn't write because I thought it was over, our . . . our affair.'

'I thought it was too,' he admitted, his lips slanting in a slightly cynical smile. 'But it wasn't and it isn't.' He raised his wine-glass to her. 'Here's to us, love.'

'Here's to us,' she whispered. The familiar excitement was beginning to throb through her. Their eyes transmitting messages to each other which their voices were refusing to speak, they both sipped their wine.

Rick looked away first to frown down at his wine glass.

'I got your address three weeks ago,' he said, 'from Sylvester, when I was in Dorada. You'd written it in the hotel register there, so I was able to send you an invitation to the exhibition.' His frown deepened as he glanced at her again. 'What did you mean when you said the sculptures of Emily aren't quite what you expected?'

'You said in Dorada . . . that you wanted to tell the story of Emily in sculpture, and I suppose I expected to see something more complicated . . . sort of scenes from her life with more figures.'

'They do tell the story of her life—her emotional life.'

'I understand that now,' she murmured, looking down at her glass, her cheeks beginning to glow in reaction to the way he was looking at her. 'I find them frightening.'

'Why?'

'I suppose it's because I know they're not Emily Greville but me.' She glanced up at him. 'It's a strange feeling, a little spooky.'

'You're identifying with the emotions,' he said quietly. 'So is every other woman who's seen them. Those figures represent not just you or Emily, but Everywoman—all the women who have experienced hope, passion or grief.'

'I heard someone say they're the best thing you've done and that you were inspired.'

'They *are* the best thing I've done, and I was inspired,' he agreed, taking her empty glass and walking over to the table by the window to put both glasses down on the tray. 'I was inspired by Emily's ghost. She haunted me until I'd told the story of her love, her passion and her grief.'

'You were in love with her,' Lori accused, and he swung round to face her.

'Perhaps I was,' he agreed. 'But I'm not any more. I've exorcised her ghost by creating those sculptures and now she's free to rest.' He walked towards her slowly, stopping when he was standing very close to her. He looked down at her, desire flickering flame-like in his eyes. 'And now that Emily's story is told, now that her ghost is laid, will you come and live with me again?'

'Where?' she asked.

'On Dorada, in Mexico—anywhere I have to go.'

'For how long?'

'For as long as you wish,' he whispered, coming closer, his breath stirring the tendrils of hair which curled on her high white forehead. 'For ever.'

She looked up, her eyes searching his face. She was close to him, not quite touching him, and it was hard to resist the pull of his physical magnetism. She wanted to rest her head against his chest, listen to the steady beat of his heart. She wanted to feel the warmth and comfort of his arms, but before she could there were questions to be answered.

'You mean it when you say for ever?' she asked.

'I mean it,' Rick answered softly, and stroked a finger down her cheek slowly and suggestively. 'Will you marry me, Lori?'

She stepped back from him, staring in amazement. She had never thought to have heard him make such a request.

'But ... but you ... you once said you found marriage too restrictive,' she exclaimed.

'I know I did.' The slant of his lips mocked himself. 'But that was how I felt when I was younger, before I'd achieved my ambition to be a sculptor, before I'd met you and had learned to love you.' He bent his head and brushed his lips across hers in a tantalising promise of a kiss. 'All the time we've been apart, even though miles have separated us and I wasn't exactly sure where you lived, I've felt close to you. It made me feel good to know you were alive somewhere in the world, going about your work, and that when I'd finished those sculptures, I'd be able to see you again and ask you to marry me.' He paused again, frowning a little as if searching for words to express himself. 'There were many nights when I wished to God I'd asked you to go with me to Mexico instead of letting you go back to Canada,' he added, his voice rasping harshly.

'Why didn't you ask me to go with you?'

'I knew I had no right to ask you,' he replied gruffly. 'And then I wasn't sure how you felt about me. You'd never told me.'

'I thought you knew,' she muttered defensively. 'I thought you knew that I wouldn't have made love with you unless I loved you. Oh, I wanted so much to go with you to Mexico—I wanted so badly for you to ask me to stay with you.'

'Then why the hell didn't you say so?' he demanded, taking her shoulders and drawing her towards him until they were close again.

'Because I knew I had no right to ask you to

take me with you. We'd made no commitment to each other. And then there was always Emily between us,' she said, touching him at last, no longer able to resist sliding her hands up over the smooth cotton of his shirt, feeling the warmth of his skin through its thinness.

'I don't understand,' he said, frowning at her, covering one of her hands with one of his, lifting it from his chest and kissing it.

'She obsessed you,' she whispered, resting her forehead against him, hearing his heart change its beat, smelling the healthy male scents of his skin. 'Sometimes when you made love to me I used to think you were making love to her. Then often you were so detached, as if . . . as if the artist part of you was standing off, watching my reactions to your kisses, storing them up in your memory to be taken out at a later date and thought about when you were doing the sculptures.'

Rick was silent for a few moments, but his arms slid about her and he held her closely, his arms warm and comforting as she had remembered them.

'I guess you're right,' he said with a sigh after a while. 'I was obsessed by Emily and perhaps when I first knew you I did think of you as being her. But it wasn't Emily who haunted me while I was in Mexico. It was you.' Under her chin his fist was rough and hard, forcing her head back so he could see her face. 'You haven't given me an answer yet. Is there someone else?' he demanded harshly, his eyes glittering with jealousy. 'Have you found another Mark to marry? Or is it your job? Do you prefer your job to living with me? If so, say so and we'll put an end to this. We'll kiss and part, go our different ways.'

'No, no, there isn't anyone else. I love you and I want to live with you always, for ever,' Lori cried urgently, roused at last. 'I didn't want to love you, but I do—I can't help it. And I don't prefer working to living with you. I hate working for other people. I want to be free, free to live with you, free to love you. I was going to Dorada this week for my spring holiday if I hadn't come here. I was hoping to see you again there.'

'You can still go to Dorada this week,' he said. 'With me. And we'll be married there soon. I know I'm not much of a catch as a husband,' he continued, with a touch of self-mockery. 'I'm untidy, often absentminded, sometimes rude and overbearing. . . .'

'Temperamental, up one day, down the next, unpredictable,' Lori teased him gently, touching his cheek in an affectionate gesture, feeling her love for him swelling up within her, coming straight from her heart. 'But always kind and generous to a fault.'

'And I love you more than I've ever loved anyone, my sweet shy love,' he said, hugging her again. 'And I want to take care of you, have you there in the morning when I wake up, take you to bed with me at night. I'd like for us to have children and to bring them up together. Lori,' he was suddenly and surprisingly humble, 'will you take the risk and marry me?'

'I'll take the risk. I'll marry you.' Her love for him burst through the bonds she had imposed upon it, sweeping away the last vestiges of her shyness. Flinging her arms about him, she pulled his head down close to hers and they kissed deeply, greedily.

'So what was that you were saying about feeling I'm making love to Emily when I'm making love to you?' Rick growled menacingly in her ear as he lifted her and carried her to the bed. 'I think the time has come for me to prove you wrong and to make damned sure you never feel like that again, don't you?'

'Yes, I do, I do,' she whispered, her arms reaching to him again, and as she surrendered blissfully to the touch of his desire she knew that the ghost of Emily Greville was no longer between them. Rick was hers, wholly hers, passionate and possessive but tender too, anticipating her sensual needs and taking time to rouse her to a passion which matched his own.

Three weeks later, in the garden behind the sugar mill on Dorada not far from the ruins of Emily Greville's house, where small brown and cream goats munched on grass and the long spears of crimson chaconia flowers swayed against the golden-brown walls of the mill, and palm trees rustled in the trade wind, they were married in a simple ceremony. Lori's foster-parents were present, and so was Kathy. Joan and Luigi Bianco were there, and so was Sylvester, and other friends Rick had made while he had been living on Dorada.

It was a joyous, somewhat hilarious occasion. At the last minute Rick couldn't find the wedding ring he had bought for her and had to borrow Joan Bianco's, and Lori was so nervous that she said his name backwards, putting his middle name, Jonathan, first and the Patrick second.

But they made no mistakes with the promises they made to each other, because they both meant every word they said, speaking from the depths of their feelings for each other, straight from their hearts.

Harlequin Plus

A WORD ABOUT THE AUTHOR

Ever since she can remember, Flora Kidd has cherished a longing to sail the seas—not on a big ocean liner, but in a sailboat. This great love brought her into contact with her husband-to-be, Wilf, who shared her dream. And over the years, they and their four children have sailed the waters of the Old World and the New (today they make their home in New Brunswick, one of Canada's maritime provinces).

Flora's decision to write came about while she was living in a seaside village in the south of Scotland. Looking for something to read, she borrowed several romance novels and afterward remarked to a friend, "I think I could write a story like these." To which the friend replied, "Maybe you could, but would anyone want to read it?"

That was the necessary challenge! Flora's first Romance, *Nurse at Rowanbank* (#1058), was published in 1966 and her first Presents, *Dangerous Pretence* (#212), appeared in 1977. She is now a best-selling author of more than twenty Romances and fifteen Presents.

A Harlequin
ROBERTA LEIGH
Collector's Edition

A specially designed collection of six exciting love stories by one of the world's favorite romance writers—Roberta Leigh, author of more than 60 bestselling novels!

1 **Love in Store** 4 **The Savage Aristocrat**
2 **Night of Love** 5 **The Facts of Love**
3 **Flower of the Desert** 6 **Too Young to Love**

Available now wherever paperback books are sold, or available through Harlequin Reader Service. Simply complete and mail the coupon below.